BLOOD IN THE FOUNTAIN

ALAN BROWN

This is a work of fiction. Names, characters, places, and incidents are products of the author's imagination or are used fictitiously and are not to be construed as real. Any resemblance to actual events, locations, organizations, or persons, living or dead, is entirely coincidental.

World Castle Publishing, LLC
Pensacola, Florida
Copyright © Alan Brown 2022
Hardback ISBN: 9798367444551
Paperback ISBN: 9781960076021
eBook ISBN: 9781960076038
First Edition World Castle Publishing, LLC, December 19, 2022
http://www.worldcastlepublishing.com
Cover: Karen Fuller
Editor: Karen Fuller

CHAPTER 1
SCHOOL OF THE OZARKS

The view from Justin Wade's dormitory room was spectacular, especially at sunset. The sun setting behind the mountains emitted a glow of warm colors that blanketed the surrounding hills. The cool lake water below collided with the warm late summer air to produce a thin layer of fog that glowed when struck by the day's last rays of sunshine.

Both the hills and the lake were backdrops to the cascading fountain that was the centerpiece of the campus. The fountain shot streams of water thirty feet in the air that arced and fell back into a large man-made pond sending ripples of water to the edges of the pond. At night, the fountain was illuminated with dozens of bright, white lights that followed the streams of water and illuminated their every movement.

The white lights from the fountain shot into Justin's room through his window. He had curtains that would have dulled the light, but he never used them. The light from the fountain was soft. It relaxed him. There was a warmth to the lights that comforted him and made him a little less homesick.

The Ozarks had a quiet elegance, particularly as the day changed to night. It was a majestic place. It was a place where people came to get away from the fast pace of life. But, for Justin, it was a lonely place.

He had only been away from home for two weeks. He hadn't made friends yet. He missed his mother's cooking. He missed the smell of his father's pipe in the family room. He missed the laughter. He was even beginning to miss his little brother. Brian was six years younger than Justin, and he was constantly getting into his stuff, especially his baseball card collection. Justin had hidden it numerous times, but his brother always seemed to find it. He had all the cards separated by team, with the players sorted based on their rookie year from oldest to newest.

All the cards were kept in one large shoe box. Brian always put the cards away in the same spot he found them. But Justin knew the instant he opened the box if his brother had gotten to them. The cards were out of order, a player was in the wrong team's stack, or the rubber band he carefully tied around each team's players was not double tied like Justin always did.

The two had argued many times over that card collection. Justin wasn't sure why, but he missed his younger brother.

He had looked forward to going away to college for so long. He thought that he was ready for his freedom, his independence. He never realized how lonely he would be away from his friends and family, away from Elise.

He and Elise had dated during his senior year. She was a junior. They had met while Justin was working at Taco Bell. They often worked the late shift together on weekends. They became friends first and then began dating. She was smart, funny and attractive.

Justin was quiet, reserved and a bit of an introvert. Elise was the exact opposite. She brought out the best in him. She was Justin's first love. He fell hard for her. His feelings were not reciprocated. She thought of Justin as more of a friend. He hoped that they would continue dating when he went away to college. But she wanted to move on. She didn't want to be tied down to a boy hundreds of miles away, whom she would see only occasionally. Justin was devastated. But he didn't let it show, not to Elise anyway.

He had left his family, friends and girlfriend for a place that seemed so isolated, so lonely.

Days were tolerable. He had classes and was surrounded by people. He was not alone. But nights were agonizing. He was in a tiny, cold, dark dormitory room by himself. The person he talked to in student housing said he was lucky. He had been assigned a room by himself. He wouldn't be crowded. He wouldn't need to share the one desk that every room had.

But he didn't feel lucky. If he had a roommate, he wouldn't be so lonely. He might even have a friend.

The light from the fountain that came through his window made him feel a little less lonely. It helped him get through the night.

The storm that night came out of nowhere. Justin was asleep when it started. A bolt of lightning followed by a crash of thunder right outside his window woke him up. Baseball-size hail pelted the campus just before midnight. The rain came down sideways with such force that it sounded like an earthquake as it crashed against the windows of the Rowlison dormitory. The hail cracked windows. The wind toppled branches. Then came a loud pop, a crackling noise from outside the window. The lights suddenly went out. The campus went dark. Even the auxiliary power failed to turn on. It was eerily dark, with only the narrow light of flashlights and the floating light from candles providing any distinction between darkness and civilization.

Students left their rooms to roam the hallways, fearful that their windows would give way to the onslaught of hail and pounding rain. Truth be told, everyone was a little afraid. Justin was no exception. He opened the door to his room and walked into the hallway. It was comforting to be in a group, to not be alone until the storm passed.

Justin had very little in common with most of the students at School of the Ozarks. He was a city boy, living his entire life in the Kansas suburbs of Kansas City. Most of the other students grew up in rural Missouri or Arkansas. Most were poor. Most enjoyed the simple side of life, fishing, hunting, and drinking. Justin grew up in a middle-class family. He had only fished once in his life and had never gone hunting. He enjoyed what the city had to offer, malls, fast food restaurants, baseball and football and plenty of movie theatres. The Ozarks offered none of those things. He was like a fish out of water.

S of O, as the students called it, was a self-sustaining college deep in the Ozarks, just ten miles from the Arkansas border. It was a college dedicated to Christian values, hard work and self-sufficiency. About 500 students attended the school, and all received a free education in exchange for work. Students worked a minimum of twenty-hours per week to pay for their tuition and room and board. Most students worked additional hours to pay for incidentals.

The student body consisted predominantly of young men and women that had struggled in life. Most were first-generation college students. Their parents couldn't afford a traditional education for their children. S of O, to them, was a blessing. Only about one in eight students who applied for admission to the school were accepted. S of O was very selective, choosing the very best students to fit in their structured, Christian environment.

Church, work and education, very much in that order, were the focal points of campus life. Freedoms were limited. Students could not have cars on campus. There was a student lot provided off-campus. It was locked from 10pm to 8am every night. Dormitories were locked at 10pm on weekdays and 11pm on weekends. Students had to be in their rooms when the dormitory was locked down. There were dress codes that required women to wear dresses and men to were slacks or khakis with button-down shirts. Men's hair could not touch their ears and could not hang below their foreheads. Attendance at Church services on Wednesday nights and Sunday mornings was required.

Attendance at all classes and school-sponsored events was mandatory unless there was an excused absence.

Rules were strict, and punishment for breaking them was stricter. Expulsions were a common punishment.

S of O was a no-nonsense college. It was a privilege to be accepted, and to get a quality, free education. Graduates had little trouble getting jobs, although most job offers tended to come from businesses in the southwest portion of the State, in or near the Ozarks.

Most students conformed to the rules and conduct standards that the school required. They realized what a wonderful opportunity the school had given them. Some, a small minority of the student body, resisted conformity. Usually, they were weeded out in a short period of time.

Every student was assigned a job on campus during their first day of orientation. Many worked in jobs they had experience with, and some worked in jobs they had an aptitude for. All had been selected first for their Christian values and secondly for their ability to fill needs in a campus job that had an opening.

S of O was unique from any other college in that the campus was completely self-sufficient. It didn't rely on outside services. Everything needed to operate the school was done on campus. Even more so than that, the school sold products they developed to outside stores and businesses. They generated considerable revenue from those sales.

The school was quite a tourist attraction. Nestled just south of Branson and the Silver Dollar City resort areas, S of O was a popular place to visit. It had a very popular restaurant on campus, a large general store that sold items made on campus, and a bakery and ice cream shop that sold items made fresh by students. It had a Christian bookstore and a small bed and breakfast that was booked months in advance. The entire tourist area was contained on the northern edge of campus, away from the dormitories, classrooms and work areas.

On Sundays, tourists flocked to campus for a church service dedicated just to them. Students attended church at 7am on Sundays. At 11am, a special service took place at the large stone church near the center of campus.

That service was for visitors and alumni only. Colorful flowers were brought in to ordain every corner of the church. The student choir, in full gowns, was present. The service took on a spirit reminiscent of a fine televangelist service. The entire service was a production designed to impress the visitors into giving large donations and departing with some of their disposable income. It worked very effectively. The campus restaurant and stores were packed for the remainder of Sunday afternoons.

The school's administration was a genius at marketing. Sure, they gave their students and their parents exactly what they promised, a quality, Christian-based education centered around a strong work ethic. But first and foremost, they sold a utopian view of life on campus. The school's reputation was impeccable, and they did whatever was necessary to keep it that way.

From an outsider's point of view, S of O appeared remarkable. They had their own police and fire departments, an electrical plant on campus provided all the needed electricity and even sold the excess back to local communities. They had a sprawling farm that raised cattle, hogs, chickens and turkeys that were slaughtered to provide food for the students while excess meat was sold to local restaurants and grocery stores. They raised vegetables and fruit trees and had the largest dairy farm in the area. The campus had its own canning facility and a large pond where they raised catfish that were harvested and appeared on the menu at the campus restaurant. There was a tailor shop that made clothes that were sold in their gift shop. Every job on campus was done by students. It was like no other college in America.

Every job had a purpose. That was to make the campus self-sufficient. Whatever products and services generated beyond what the campus needed to function were sold back to the surrounding communities and to the visitors and guests that flocked to the campus.

The school had accumulated great wealth over the years, but it was a quiet wealth. It was a wealth that few people knew about. The image they portrayed was that of a struggling college in desperate need of donations and support. From the outside, the campus looked worn, outdated, and in need of repair. That was exactly the image they wanted outsiders to have of S of O.

Donations came into the school from all over the country. It was a college that people wanted to believe in. It provided free education to students that desperately needed it. But, more than that, S of O provided education to the right students, the cream of the crop, the students that were most deserving, the students that would make good citizens and good Christians.

S of O was a success story like no other. They had worked hard to groom their reputation, and they worked equally hard to maintain it.

There was always a darkness that was behind the façade that the administration tried so hard to maintain. It was a darkness that crept through the underbelly of campus life. It was a darkness that few knew anything about. It was a darkness that Justin Wade soon would discover.

Justin came to S of O because he had nowhere else to go. His parents couldn't afford to send him to college. His father had been sick for some time, a heart attack, followed by another, followed by a minor stroke. He hadn't been able to work for nearly a year. His mother had taken a secretarial job to make ends meet.

A year earlier, Justin figured he'd get an athletic scholarship that would pay for all or most of his college education. Several college coaches were talking to him. He was a star long-distance runner on his high school cross-country and track teams. He had done well at regionals and State in his junior year. He had finished a successful cross-country season his senior year. Everything looked bright. He had been a guest at the University of Kansas. Coach Simmons said that he would be a great addition to their teams. A full scholarship was in his grasp.

Then, a serious illness landed him in the hospital. An inflammation around his heart would take months to fully heal. His scholarship hopes disappeared.

There was one hope. Justin had read an article about the School of the Ozarks. The article told of the school providing a free education. It also mentioned that they had a very successful sports program. Their cross-country team had been to the NAIA Nationals for six consecutive years. He contacted S of O's track and cross-country coach and scheduled a visit.

The school did not give out athletic scholarships, although they did reduce work requirements for student athletes. There was one big catch, though. Justin would need to go through the same process as all the other applicants for acceptance. He had to get a recommendation letter from his minister. He had to provide recommendations from his principal, employer, and five others. His parents would need to show tax returns and provide financial information to show that they could not afford to pay for college tuition.

Justin completed everything that was required, and then he waited. Two months went by. Finally, Coach Moffit phoned him.

"You've been accepted, Justin," he said. "You need to be here August 3 to get set up and begin cross-country training."

The day Justin was scheduled to leave for school, Elise showed up to say goodbye. He hoped she would, but he didn't expect it. After all, they had agreed to part ways when he left for college. He packed his '73 cherry red Volkswagen Beetle, said goodbye to his parents, gave Elise a final, tearful kiss and drove the nearly 200 miles south to S of O.

His first impression of the campus at S of O was that he had gone back in time. He nearly turned around when he saw the large iron gates that marked the entrance to campus. They were closed when he approached them. A security guard came to his car, asked his name, checked a list and opened the gates. That made him anxious about what might be awaiting him behind those gates. The white stone building and the gravel roads that led down to the dormitories looked like something out of the early 20th century. It had the look of a prison and feel of a prison. He thought several times that he had made a mistake. He considered turning around and going back home. But he didn't.

He settled in his dormitory room later that day. Justin had been assigned to Rowlison Hall, the oldest of the two men's dormitories. All freshmen and sophomores were assigned to that dormitory. It was nearly 80 years old, had no air conditioning and was reminiscent of a large, brick psychiatric hospital that one might expect to see in a 60s horror movie.

Paint was peeling from the walls. All the floors were a dull, faded, ugly brown shade of linoleum. The ceilings were tall. The lighting was poor. To Justin, Rowlison Hall was a depressing place.

There were six stories to the dormitory. Justin was assigned to room 613. There were no elevators, so he had to unload his car and carry everything up six flights of stairs. His room was small, maybe 10' X 12'. Inside was one bunk bed and one desk and chair. There were no individual bathrooms. Each floor had a large group shower. There were a dozen shower heads, six urinals and six toilet stalls. It reminded Justin of his high school athletic locker room.

"*It looks and feels like a reform school,*" he wrote his mother two days after arriving on campus,

In reality, Justin though of S of O as more like a prison than a reform school. But he didn't want to frighten his mother by saying that in a letter.

Curfew was 10pm on weeknights and 11pm on weekends. The doors to Rowlison Hall were locked at precisely those times. Hallway lights were turned down at 10:30pm and 11:30pm, respectively. Students were only allowed to leave their room for work assignments or to use the bathroom after the lights were turned down.

Justin received his work assignment the second day he was on campus. He was assigned to the Ozark Family Restaurant. It was the visitor and guest restaurant at the entrance to campus. Justin had a unique talent that was in need at the restaurant. He could drive a stick shift. The Volkswagen he drove was a three-speed stick shift. That talent came in handy at the restaurant. Supplies and deliveries for the restaurant and the adjacent gift shop were made in a 10-year-old, beat-up Ford van with a standard transmission and a challenging stick-shift.

He soon discovered that the delivery van was every bit as temperamental as his beetle had been when he first learned to drive it. But, in a short time, he was able to drive it without it stalling out or jumping with every shift.

Making deliveries and picking up supplies was an easy job. Others loaded the van, and others emptied it. All he had to do was drive ten hours a week, most of that on weekends. His deliveries enabled him to see how vast the campus was. Most people had no idea how much acreage S of O owned. They had quietly accumulated hundreds of acres of surrounding land over the years, stretching to the mountains on two sides and including most of the valley area nestled between three lakes.

The dairy was located in the far northeast corner of campus, down a winding dirt road, with fields of corn, wheat, barley and soy on either side. About a mile onto the dirt road was a large wire fence with a gate. It was locked. Justin had been given a key to unlock it. The wire fence ran the entire perimeter of the campus. Until Justin's first delivery to the dairy farm, he had assumed the wire fence marked the end of S of O's property line.

He was wrong. The school's property extended far past the wire fences.

The dairy farm was huge, extending another two miles or so beyond the wire fence. There was something else odd that Justin noticed about the dairy farm. The workers were older. They weren't students. He had been told that all work positions on the S of O campus were filled by students. But that wasn't the case at the dairy.

To the north of the dairy farm were the transportation building and lot. S of O had its own fleet of school buses and vans that were used for school travel, mainly by the athletic department for transporting athletes to various events.

Cross-country training began the second day he was on campus. Coach Moffit had arranged for his work assignments to be flexible so as not to interfere with practice or classes. S of O was accommodating in that regard. Every job on campus worked around classes, athletic schedules and church.

A strong Christian education was promised by S of O to all prospective students and their parents. The church near the campus center was the centerpiece of their Christian education. The church was non-denominational but had the feel of an evangelical doctrine. Every student was required to take four years of religion classes. In addition, all students had to attend two church services every week, one on Wednesday night and the other on Sunday morning. The campus church was massive. The exterior was made from the same white stone as the rest of the buildings on campus. The interior was made of fine cherry wood and local oak. It could accommodate a congregation of a thousand or more. 24-stain glass windows on each side, a vestibule the size of a small house, and a steeple that towered above all other buildings on campus.

Coach Moffit's team was loaded with stellar athletes. There were seven athletes on the school's cross-country team. All were strong runners. The team consisted of two State High School Champions.

Brad Connelly was a sophomore. He had been the Louisiana Class 4A cross-country champion. He was built low-to-the ground, 5'4" maybe, with thick, muscular legs, heavier-looking than most long-distance runners but not an ounce of fat. Every bit of his body was muscular. He believed in weight-training, and it showed. He had short, brown hair, trimmed close to the scalp on the sides and back with a flat-top. The top of his head looked a bit like a landing strip with thick, rigid, brown hairs on the surface.

Justin had only seen boys wearing flattops in old, black and white 50s and 60s movies and television shows. He didn't know anyone still wore their hair that way. But somehow, Brad Connelly pulled it off. He was the most dedicated runner Justin had ever met. He didn't drink alcohol. He didn't smoke. He was extremely careful about what he ate. When he wasn't in classes, he was running or in the weight room. Brad Connelly was the captain of the cross-country team.

Eric Cramer was the second of the dynamic duo. He, like, Justin, was a freshman. Eric was the Missouri Class 2A cross-country champion. Brad referred to him as "pretty boy."

He had curly, sandy hair and looked a bit like a young Mathew McConaughey. He even had the same boyish smile and laugh. He had the type of All-American good looks that caused girls to stop and stare at him as he walked past them in the halls or on the pathways through campus. But on the inside, Eric Cramer was every bit as dedicated to running as Brad Connelly. They were roommates and resided at Smith Hall. That was the newest and nicest dormitory on campus. It was reserved for upper classmen and special athletes. Coach Moffit pulled strings to get Eric Cramer in that dorm.

Two weeks into cross-country practices, Justin struggled to make friends on the cross-country team. He was different. He was a city boy. He wore his hair longer. He just didn't act or talk or have the same interests as the other members of the team. Earl Myers, a sophomore on the team, seemed to be the only one that made an effort to be friendly toward Justin. By his own admission, Earl was a good old, red-neck country boy. He grew up in the Ozark hills, not far from Branson. He grew up in a dirt floor, wood cabin, a mile from any neighbors. His dad used to work in the coal mines of Southern Missouri years early before they closed. For the last several years, he's been unemployed. His mother made homemade soap and butter. She sold them at a flea market south of Springfield to make ends meet. Earl was the first member of his family to go to college.

During the grinding cross-country workouts, Earl hung close to Justin. He talked the entire time. Once Earl referred to himself as being made up of two-thirds bullshit and one-third Ozark manure.

When Justin asked what Ozark manure was, Earl smiled and said, "It's crap that smells good."

Justin enjoyed listening to Earl talk. It kept his mind off the pain of Coach Moffit's workouts.

The coach was a believer in strength and resistance training. His workouts were brutal, two-a-days for the first three weeks. One of his favorite workouts for the team was a six-mile run over gravel roads to Outlook Mountain. That was a mountain on the edge of Branson, Missouri, that, at its peak, provided a scenic view of the tri-lakes and downtown Branson area. At the foot of the mountain were concrete stairs that went up one side of the mountain to the viewing area at the very top.

Each time the team ran to the base of Outlook Mountain, Coach Moffit was waiting for them in his old '72 Mercury. He popped the trunk when he saw the first runners approaching. Inside were weighted backpacks, each contained two concrete blocks, each weighing ten-pounds. The weight of the backpacks pushed the body back to an almost perfect vertical position. But that was a benefit of the weighted backpacks, not the purpose. The purpose was strength and resistance training. Each running ran up the 138 stairs as fast as possible. Then, at the top, each runner ran down the stairs. Twenty times up and twenty times down. It was brutal on the legs and ankles. Heart rates soared, running up the stairs. Breathing was rapid, everyone sucking deeply for air. The quadriceps of the legs tightened and ached with pain. Legs became so heavy it was a challenge to lift them to reach the next step. Once at the top, the pain was not over. Going down the stairs had unique challenges. The weighted backpacks that had kept the body vertical during the upward climb pushed the body downward going down the stairs. Justin's lower back ached with pain. He had to shift his body weight to his heals to keep from falling down the stairs.

Brad Connelly brought up the rear of the group, ensuring everyone continued running and making sure that all twenty repetitions up and down the stairs were done by all the runners. If a runner got too far behind, he was there to push them. If a runner stopped to vomit, he was there to get them going afterward.

The stairs on Outlook Mountain were absolute Hell, and once the twenty repetitions were completed and the backpacks returned to Coach Moffitt's car, there were still six miles of gravel roads to be run to get back to campus.

Three workouts every week involved strength and resistance training. Each was followed the next day by a long, slow, twelve to fifteen-mile run. Every resistance workout Coach Moffit planned seemed more sadistic than the other to Justin.

There was the one that he used on rainy, miserable days when the team worked out indoors. Coach Moffit had seven treadmills lined up against one wall of the gym. Something that looked like a bungee cord was attached to the far wall on the other side of the gym. At the end of the bungee cord was a harness. Each runner wrapped the harness around their shoulders and upper body. The coach turned each treadmill on to a slow, jogging pace, and when he blew his whistle, each runner ran to the treadmill. The resistance from the bungee cord took effect about ten feet before the treadmill. It took incredible effort to stretch the cord far enough to get fully on the treadmill. Then, with each runner struggling to maintain a pace while the bungee cord pulled their body backward, Coach Moffit blew his whistle, signaling for everyone to increase the speed of their treadmill one-mile per hour. The whistle would blow several times. Then, satisfied that the first repetition had been done the way he wanted, Coach Moffit blew the whistle twice, and the runners came off the back for a two-minute rest before the next repetition.

The first time Justin did the workout, when he slowed to rest, the bungee cord snapped his body backward twelve feet, and he landed on the hard, wood gym floor.

On yet another resistance training workout, Coach Moffit divided the team into two separate teams, four on one and three on the other. He took the two teams out to the 400-meter, oval cinder track where two sleighs were waiting, each with harnesses that wrapped around the shoulders and upper body. The sleighs, about the size of a child's wagon, had two metal bars that ran along the bottom. They ran along the front and back edges of the sleigh in resistance to the track. Inside, they were weighted down with fifty pounds of concrete blocks. Each team member would run one lap and hand off the harness and sleigh to the next teammate. The race would go one for a hundred laps or approximately twenty-five miles. The winning team typically got two miles trimmed off of their evening cool-down run.

The team with only three members had considerably more mileage to run than the other team. Coach called that the "Garbage" team. They were the three runners that the coach felt hadn't lived up to his expectations during the earlier week's workouts.

Every resistance workout was followed by a six-mile run to cool down. Brad Connelly led the run and set the pace. Eric Cramer brought up the rear to make sure all the runners completed their workout.

The intensity of Coach Moffit's workouts was much greater than anything Justin had experienced in high school. They left him exhausted and in terrible pain. His leg muscles tightened up at night, making it difficult to walk. After dinner, he went to his room, did homework and went straight to bed. But the workouts were paying off. Justin was in the best shape he had ever been in. His heart was strong, and his legs were running harder and faster than any time before.

The first few weeks at S of O had been a lonely experience for Justin. Work, run, and sleep was what every day consisted of.

That's where he found himself on the stormy night two weeks into his stay at S of O. A nearby lightning strike knocked the power off on campus. The lights were out in Rowlison Hall, and most of the students, flashlights in hand, gathered in the corridor outside their rooms. After thirty minutes or so, the storm began to let up. The wind was no longer howling. The thunder was softer now, more distant. Finally, the lights began to flicker and then they came back on. Students headed back to their rooms. So did Justin.

There was something different in his room this time. The light from the fountain across the way from his window was not on.

The fountain must not have gotten its power back yet, he thought.

Justin lay in bed, trying to relax, trying to forget about the pain in his quadriceps and shins that were pounding, trying to go to sleep.

Suddenly, there was a loud grinding noise coming from outside the window. The white lights from the pond began to shine through his window. But the noise was odd. It sounded like a motor tearing into something, trying to keep going and work past whatever was in its way.

Then the sound softened. Justin closed his eyes, not tightly, just enough to soften the rays of white light that were glowing in his eyes from the fountain. That's when he noticed it. Something was different. The light had changed. It was no longer white.

He opened his eyes. Rays of pink light slowly changed to red until his entire room was blanked in a red color. He jumped to his feet and went to the window.

Across the way were the pond and the fountain. Spraying out of the fountain was a red color that looked very much like blood.

CHAPTER 2
BODIES IN THE POND

The power to the fountain was shut off ten-minutes later. Justin watched from his window as men with flashlights moved around the pond. The overcast sky that night hid the moon and made it impossible to see what was going on at the pond. But based on the number of flashlights, he could assume there were at least a dozen people around the pond.

Justin was curious. He wanted to know what was going on at the pond. He grabbed his binoculars, the ones his mother had given him last Christmas and opened the window to his room. The ledge outside was about two feet wide. The fire escape was less than six feet from his window. He climbed onto the ledge, walked carefully to the fire escape and went down the ladder.

If he was caught out after curfew, he would face expulsion, so he moved slowly and quietly so as not to be seen or heard by anyone else. When he reached the ground, he took the backway around to the pond, the way that would take him through a wooded area that he hoped would hide him from view. About seventy-five feet from the pond, he stopped, took a crouched position behind a bush and lifted the binoculars to his eyes. He adjusted them several times to get them in focus.

There were several uniformed officers holding flashlights on the opposite side of the pond, nearest the fountain. On the pond near the fountain were three row boats with one man inside each. Someone appeared to be in the water. Then an object surfaced from the area beneath the fountain. Whatever the object was appeared to be large. Two men were attempting to pull it to one of the boats. He focused his binoculars on that area of the water.

In a few minutes, he saw a diver appear on the water's surface. Then another. They were puling something to the surface. Justin saw a large canvas with ropes tied around it. Out of one edge of the canvas was a leg with a tennis shoe on the end.

Then two other divers surfaced next to another boat. They pulled up a second canvas with ropes tied around it. Justin's hands and legs began to shake. His heart began to race. Justin had never seen a dead body before. It was unnerving.

The first glow of sunlight was on the eastern horizon. It was nearly 5am. The sun would be coming over the horizon soon. Justin put the binoculars back in his pocket and hurried back to the dormitory, to the fire escape.

Justin was shaken by what he had seen. Two bodies wrapped and tied in canvases being pulled from the pond. He wanted to tell someone, anyone, what he had seen. But he couldn't. Afterall, he had broken curfew when he left the dormitory in the middle of the night.

Besides, he thought, *the news will be all over campus in a few hours. Hell, it will be all over the local news, maybe even the national news.*

When he returned to his room, he put the binoculars away, got a change of clothes and headed to the shower.

"The dining hall opened at 6am," he reasoned. *"By the time he showered and changed clothes, it would be nearly that time. The dormitory doors would be unlocked, and he could safely walk by the pond to see what was happening."*

There will probably be a crowd gathering close to the pond by then, he thought. *People will be curious about the large group of police officers.*

Justin left Rowlison Hall, turned left out of the front doorway, looked to the pond and stopped in his tracks. He couldn't believe his eyes.

No one was at the pond. The campus police were gone. The row boats on the water were gone. There was no sign that anything unusual had happened at the pond. The fountain was running again, shooting clear water high in the air.

He went to the dining hall that day, attended classes, and talked to classmates. There was no mention of the bodies that had been pulled out of the pond. The newspaper did not mention anything. Neither did the television news. It was as if nothing had happened. The few people that knew what happened weren't telling anyone.

Justin even questioned what he had seen. Maybe he was wrong.

The death of two people in the campus pond couldn't have been kept quiet, he thought. *Maybe I didn't actually see two bodies. It was dark outside. I was a long way away. The binoculars I used did not have a strong magnification lens,* he rationalized.

In a few days, Justin put the incident at the pond in the back of his mind. He had classes, training and work to concentrate on. Besides, he had met someone.

Her name was Risa Thompson. She was beautiful. Long flowing, thick brown hair with big blue eyes and long eyelashes. But it was her smile that hooked him. She had large, thick lips and a contagious smile that caused her lips to puff up and her dimples to jump. She had a look of innocence to her that girls from the city rarely displayed. But she wasn't like the girls on campus that came from the hills and Ozarks of southwest Missouri. She had a sophistication to her. She spoke without the southern Missouri accent that was so prevalent on campus.

Justin first noticed her when he was walking through

campus on one of the main walkways leading from the classrooms to the dormitories. She was alone, walking from the fine arts building back toward student housing. He was walking to his next class. He saw her in the distance wearing a red, flowery dress that flowed down below her knees. It was a conservative dress that left a lot to his imagination, but he could tell by the way she wore that dress, the way she walked, that she was something special.

He slowed his walk as she approached. When their eyes met, they both smiled. Hers was a big smile that stretched from one corner of her face to the other. His was a sheepish grin that boys tend to have when they are caught staring at a girl that they don't intend her to see them looking. She said, "hi," as they passed each other. He tried to get a "hi" out, but his mouth was dry, and the word became a soft whisper that he was certain she didn't hear.

For two days, he thought of the girl. Everywhere he went, he looked for her. Then fate brought them together. He had been assigned an early Sunday morning shift at the Ozark Restaurant to make deliveries and pick-up bread, pastries and desserts from the campus bakery that the restaurant would need that day. He headed to the bakery first thing that morning. He pulled up at the dock behind the bakery and went inside.

That's when he saw her again. She was working in the campus bakery. He approached her while his truck was being loaded.

"Hi, I'm Justin," he said with a sheepish grin.

"Nice to meet you, Justin," she said with a broad smile. "I'm Risa. You didn't grow up from around here, did you, Justin?"

"No, how did you guess that?" he asked.

"You don't have a southern accent."

"Yeah, I'm from Kansas City. How about you. You don't sound like you're from around here either."

"Well, sounds can be deceiving," she said. "I'm from the Bootheel, a place called Sikeston. So, I guess that I do come from the south, but my mother is an English teacher. She worked hard to eliminate my southern drawl."

"She did a good job," Justin said with a smile. "I've got to tell you, Risa. You've got the most beautiful eyes."

"Well, Justin. Is that a line you use with all the girls?"

"No, I'm really very shy. I don't even know any girls on campus."

"Well, that's not true. You know me now."

Justin had never seen a smile as warm as the one Risa was giving. He had never felt this way about a girl since Elise. He didn't even know her, but he knew she was special.

"You know, Justin. I've seen you running through campus. Are you on the track team?"

"Yes, cross-country too. That was the main reason I came to S of O. How about you? Why did you choose S of O?"

"I want to be a teacher. S of O has a great teaching program, and they place most of their graduates in positions right after graduation. Besides, free tuition is great."

"Yeah, that is true. Well, Risa, it was nice meeting you. I better go. I need to get the bakery items back to the restaurant."

Justin turned and started to walk away.

"Wait, Justin. Don't you want to ask me something?"

"What?" he said with a curious look.

"Don't you want to ask me out?"

"Yes, I do," he said with a huge smile. "Where would you like to go?"

"Well, do you have a car?"

"Yes."

"There's a new movie at the Branson cinema. How about picking me up Friday night about 7pm? I'm living at Claire Hall."

"It's a date. I'll see you then."

Justin was excited and nervous at the same time. Risa made him feel like no other girl he had ever met. It was an odd feeling. He didn't even know her. All week he thought about their date. He had been a loner. He had been depressed. He had been homesick ever since he arrived on campus. Now he was excited. Life on campus didn't seem so bad. Cross-country practices didn't seem as difficult. Classes were a bit more interesting. Even the food at the campus cafeteria tasted better. Risa had changed his perception. He was more outgoing.

His positive attitude had not gone unnoticed by Coach Moffit and the members of his team.

"You look like you've turned the corner, Justin," Coach told him. "Keep that positive attitude up, and you're going to do well."

His positive attitude was showing in his practices. Justin was no longer lagging toward the back of the team in his workouts. He was no longer being pushed by Eric Cramer to catch up with the pack. Now he was at the front of the pack with Brad Connelly. He was talking to his teammates, getting to know them.

"They were a good group of guys," he told himself. *"They were a team that hung together and took care of each other, and he had become part of that team."*

Besides the two leaders of the team, Brad and Eric, there was Earl Myers. He was not built like a typical long-distance runner. Earl was 6'3" and was built more like a football linebacker. He took long strides that were about twice as long as any of the other runners. He hit the ground with a force that sprayed rocks up from his heels on the gravel roads the team ran. His teammates avoided running directly behind him for fear of being hit by the rocks.

Earl was a good-old-boy from Carthage, MO. He was a sophomore and the fourth-best runner on the team. He was also crazy. He partied as hard as he ran. Earl had one speed, fast. He gave 100% to everything he did, and there wasn't a challenge that he wouldn't accept. During one practice, a long, slow twelve-mile run along the gravel roads, Daryl Coleman, another member of the team, challenged Earl to run the entire workout barefoot. So, Earl did. The rocks cut into his feet. They bled. The pain was horrendous. But Earl didn't say a word. He ran the entire workout barefoot. His feet looked like a chunk of raw hamburger afterward. Peebles and pieces of gravel were embedded in the bottoms of his feet. From his ankles down, he was coated in blood. It would take his feet weeks to completely heal. Still, he never missed a practice. He wrapped his feet tightly and ran without showing a glimpse of pain.

Earl was Justin's best friend on the team, although he wasn't sure if Earl felt the same way about him. Justin had assumed that because Earl ran side-by-side with him during most workouts and talked to him the entire way, he must have considered Justin a good friend. But when Brad came up to Justin after practice one day and told him, "Thanks for putting up with Earl. Nobody else on the team can stand to listen to him talk the entire practice," Justin couldn't help but wonder if Earl spent time with him only because no one else wanted to listen to him.

Another obnoxious habit that Earl had was screaming out when he ran. He would scream at the top of his lungs whenever he felt his body slowing down. The screams would energize him. His pace would pick up. In nearly every workout and every race, the team could count on hearing at least one long, agonizing scream come from him.

The first time Justin heard the scream, he froze in his tracks. It sounded like someone was dying ahead of him.

"Keep running, kid," Eric Cramer said. "It's just Earl."

Daryl Coleman was the only senior on the team. He was the easy-going member of the team. Nothing seemed to bother him. He ran because it made him feel good. He did not have a competitive bone in his body. But he had a love for running, for being out in nature. Nothing seemed to get under his skin except maybe Earl Myers. He was the exact opposite of Earl. He didn't care about medals. He didn't care about improving his performance. He simply liked to run. Earl was so excitable. He was the team motivator and the team cheerleader. He challenged everyone to do better. But Daryl was different. He was not going to be forced or pushed into doing more than he wanted to do. He was a pacifist. Earl was a warrior.

He would find ways to get to Earl, normally through a silly challenge he knew his teammate could not refuse.

Dennis Glenn was another member of the team. He was a freshman. Like Justin, he was from Kansas. Also, like Justin, he once aspired to get a scholarship with the University of Kansas. A torn Achilles tendon in his junior year ended that dream.

Dennis came to S of O because he had heard they had an outstanding coach who could rehabilitate almost any injury. His recovery had been slow, though. His Achilles tendon still bothered him. At night he massaged it and used plenty of ice to keep the swelling down. Before each workout, he spent thirty minutes in the hot tub, then rubbed a substance called atomic balm on his leg. His body sweat activated the ointment and caused it to heat up, soaking into his skin down to his tendons and causing them to warm up and relax. After rubbing the ointment on, he wrapped his ankle tightly with an elastic bandage.

Dennis convinced Justin to try atomic balm for his sore muscles. He had a mild case of shin splints. The first time he tried it, his skin felt like it was on fire. It was so intense that it removed the hair on his legs from underneath the balm.

"Just a little bit will do the trick," Dennis had said.

He couldn't imagine needing to put it on every day just to endure a workout.

Justin felt empathy for Dennis. Not only had Dennis had

an injury that ended his high school running, but, like Justin, he
had lost his scholarship opportunity as a result. And, more than
that, Dennis was enduring incredible pain to continue running.

Dennis was the seventh runner on a seven-person team.
In cross-country competitions, each team is allowed to race seven
athletes. But only the fastest five are counted in the team score.
The place of finish of each of the first five runners to cross the
finish line is tallied to determine the team score. The lowest score
wins the competition. Dennis was an extra runner. His place in
the race rarely counted in the team score. That bothered him
immensely.

He gave 100%. He ran with as much courage and heart
as anyone on the team. But his body hadn't completely healed.
Every step he took was painful. He had no acceleration. He could
only go at the same, consistent speed. Races were nightmares to
him. He watched as other runners went past him. His mind and
body wanted to go with them, but he couldn't. His leg would not
allow it. So, time after time, he finished near the back of the pack.
Still, he didn't give up.

Bobby Cockran was the last member of the cross-country
team. He was a local boy from a small town thirty minutes
outside Branson, high in the mountains. His daddy was a Baptist
preacher. Bobby was a very religious person. He gave the team
prayer before practices and competitions. He didn't smoke.
He didn't drink. He didn't swear. He seemed to have no vices.
Bobby was the spiritual leader of the team. Running came second
to God. He loved to run. He welcomed the pain. He often said
that God tested him with the pain. Running brought him closer
to the Lord. He wasn't particularly fast, but he never gave up.
Bobby was the sixth-best runner on the team. He and Dennis
often ran together both in their workouts and in competitions.
But, in competitions, Bobby always beat Dennis. He would hang
with him until the last two hundred yards or so, then Bobby took

off.

"The spirit of the Lord goes through me like a wind at my back," he would say.

Bobby sprinted the last part of every race, usually passing several other runners to the finish line.

Coach Moffit would get upset at Bobby. *"If you can finish the race sprinting, then you're leaving too much in your gas tank,"* he would say. It didn't matter how upset the coach got. Bobby always ran the same way.

The five days before Justin's first date with Risa went by fast. Between workouts, classes and homework, the days were short. Two days before the date, the cross country workouts eased. The season's first race was Saturday, and the coach eased up on the workouts to get everyone's legs fresh for the race. The team bus would leave for the University of Missouri at Rolla at 5am on Saturday morning.

In hindsight, planning a date with Risa for Friday night might not have been the best idea. But he wasn't going to tell her that. Besides, the curfew was 11pm. He couldn't be out too late. Justin would get at least four or five hours of sleep before he had to wake up. He had run many races in the past with less sleep than that.

Friday, after practice and before the date, he showered, shaved and applied a light amount of cologne. Then, he dressed in his church slacks and a blue button-down shirt. He combed his hair and sprayed just a touch of hair spray on it to keep it in place. Then, he took a deep breath and headed to Claire Hall. He could never remember being this nervous about a date. He was perspiring. His hands were shaking.

When he entered the dormitory, Risa was waiting for him. She wore a blue sun dress with spaghetti straps that showed her beautiful, tanned skin. The dress was shorter than what he had seen her in before. It showed her legs from just above the knees down. They were firm, tan and athletic looking. They weren't skinny, but they weren't thick either. They were just right.

She smiled when she saw him walk in. They walked together through campus and up the hill to the student parking lot. She took his hand when they were nearly at the top of the hill by the front gate to the campus.

The movie that they saw was forgettable. Their date was not. Risa talked. Justin listened. He loved listening to her. She was so full of life, so incredibly positive. He was an introvert. She was an extrovert. She complemented him so well. It was only their first date. He knew so little about her. She knew so little about him. But it seemed like they had known each other for many years.

The night went by fast. They stopped at Dairy Queen for ice cream when the movie was over. Then it was time to get back to campus. The dormitories were locked at 11pm. When he pulled into the student parking lot, he turned off the ignition, reached over and pulled Risa close. He looked into her eyes, expecting her to object. She didn't. He pressed his lips against hers. It was a soft, gentle kiss. He held his lips to hers for several seconds. Her lips were sweet. When he moved his lips away, he noticed her eyes were closed, and her lips did not back away. He had the feeling that he could have continued kissing her, that she wanted him to. But he wasn't going to chance it. The night had been perfect. He didn't want to ruin it by trying to go too far.

They walked hand-in-hand back to Claire Hall. At the foot of the steps leading up to the entrance, Risa leaned over and kissed Justin on the cheek. "Good luck in your race tomorrow," she said. "I'll be waiting for you when you get back."

Justin had trouble sleeping that night. He was nervous about the race and couldn't get his mind off Risa. At 4:30am, his alarm went off. He dressed in his uniform and headed to the gym. A few minutes later, he was on the bus.

The bus the team road in was a ten-year-old school bus, painted white and burgundy for the school colors, with School of the Ozarks printed in large, burgundy colors on both sides of the bus. The seats inside were torn, with the cotton interior coming through tears in the fabric. The paint was rusting, and the floorboards had nearly rubbed through to the metal frame.

The bus was on the downward side of life. It had seen better days. The bus driver was named Tyler. He was a junior at S of O, short and thin. He looked younger than his twenty years. When everyone was loaded, Tyler started the bus. He struggled at first with the stick shift to get it in the right gear, but after one stall and a jump shifting into second gear, the bus was rolling.

The bus ride was quiet except for Earl. He seemed to talk the entire way, mostly to himself, since most of the other teammates were either asleep or trying to go to sleep.

The bus ride to Rolla was nearly three hours long. It was early in the morning, and Justin was exhausted. He took a seat as far away from Earl as he could get. Then he pulled his red cap down over his face, crouched down in the seat and tried to sleep. He wasn't very successful. Every time he dozed off, it seemed that Tyler would hit a bump or he would hear Earl talking.

By the time the bus reached the golf course in Rolla, where the race was to take place, his back ached, and his head was pounding. He was far from being ready to run.

The race was a dual meet between the University of Missouri at Rolla and S of O. UMR had twenty times the student body of S of O. On paper, UMR should have easily beat S of O. They were the larger school in a larger conference with four times the number of cross-country runners as S of O. But Coach Moffit's teams were always strong, and this year's team was one of his best.

Less than a mile into the three-mile race, Brad Connelly and Eric Cramer had separated from the pack. Eric held on to

Brad's shoulder as long as he could, but a series of hills during the last half-mile was too much for Eric to keep pace with his teammate, and Brad pulled away.

Justin was in sixth place at the halfway mark, but his legs felt good, and he was increasing his pace. He positioned himself just off the right shoulder of the Rolla runner ahead of him. When they reached a long uphill grade, Justin increased the speed of his arm swing, shortened his stride length, lowered his head and sprinted ahead. His competitor put up no resistance. He continued his speed through the downhill, closing in on another Rolla runner. He had nestled in on the competitor's right shoulder, preparing to pass him. But the Rolla harrier heard him coming. He lowered his head and began to sprint. That's when he heard it.

Earl Myer's scream was loud, long and with a defiant tone that no one this far into a cross-country race deserved to have. It was his victory scream. Brad Connelly had warned him about it. Earl liked to run from the back of the pack announcing the passing of each competitor with a loud scream. It was unnerving to the competition and energizing to his teammates.

Justin welcomed Earl's screams. They gave him strength, and they were unnerving to the competitors. Earl's scream threw off the stride of the Rolla harrier, allowing Justin to sprint past him into the fourth position.

Earl Myers screamed four more times within the next several minutes. Each scream was closer. He was closing on Justin. The last scream sounded like he was just a few yards behind.

The last scream was timely. It happened on the final sprint to the finish, no more than fifty yards. Rolla's top harrier was in a full sprint. Justin was just a step behind. Earl's scream motivated Justin. It startled the Rolla runner just enough to break his pace and allow Justin to go past him ten yards before the finish.

He didn't realize until he crossed the finish line that Earl was right behind him. He had managed to pass Rolla's top harrier giving S of O the top 4 finishes.

CHAPTER 3
NEW FRIENDSHIPS

The bus ride back to S of O was a joyous one. There was plenty of laughter and excitement over the results of the first cross-country competition of the season. Rolla was no pushover. They were a much larger school in a much larger conference with a veteran team that had fared well the last several years.

This was S of O's first test, and they had done very well. There were three more dual meets ahead of them before they moved into larger competitions. Each school they would compete against was much larger, with better training facilities and larger teams to pick their varsities from.

But Coach Moffit knew he had a special team, a strong team, maybe his best team ever. And so did every runner on the S of O team.

The athletes' dynamic on that bus changed with that race against Rolla. For the first time, they became a team, shedding any thoughts of individual success for the team's good. They would develop a bond after that first race that would change them from individuals into a brotherhood.

Cross-country was like no other sport because a team was only as strong as its weakest link or at least the fifth runner since final team scores were based on the top five team finishes. Practices would seem less tedious now and more focused on bringing the weakest runners up to their highest levels.

On that bus ride home, there was a sense that every team member was equally important to the team's success. There was a sense that they would need to bond as friends as well as teammates. As a result of that first competition, they were united in becoming a family.

Coach Moffit knew that too. Within a few days, he moved the entire team to the fifth floor of Brown Hall. They would share a four-bedroom suite with a common area. Justin couldn't believe his eyes when he first saw his new residence. It was so much nicer than anything he had seen in Rowlison Hall. The suite was large, with a carpeted common area and bathrooms in each of the four bedrooms. It was air-conditioned. The suite was freshly painted. It looked new. Each bedroom had two full-size beds, unlike the bunk beds in other dormitory rooms. There was a small kitchen with a full-size refrigerator. There was even a television set in the common area. Justin would share a room with Earl Myers.

Life at S of O was becoming much more tolerable.

"Living together, eating together, taking classes together will bring you closer," Coach Moffit told them.

There was only one thing that wasn't coming together for Justin. That was his relationship with Risa. She wasn't waiting for him when he returned from that first competition. He went to her dormitory. She wasn't there. He called her floor several times over the next few weeks. There was one common phone on each floor of the dormitory. It was frustrating to call. Many times, the phone line was busy, and sometimes no one would answer. If Justin was lucky, someone would answer and go to Risa's room to look for her. But he was always told that she wasn't there.

Justin tried to put her out of his mind. They had only had one date. Perhaps she just wasn't that into him. Besides, he had a lot on his plate now. He needed to concentrate on his training and his classes.

As Coach Moffit had anticipated, housing the team

together in Brown Hall was bonding them even more. They pushed each other both in practices and in classes. Performances were improving, and so were grades. They were a family now, spending most days and weekends together. They ate together, went to classes together and attended campus church together. Most evenings were spent together in that common room, watching television, talking and nursing sore muscles or minor injuries that resulted from the grueling workouts that Coach Moffit put them through.

His belief in long runs on back country gravel roads mixed with hill and resistance training was improving everyone's performance, but at a cost. Shin splints, pulled muscles, blistered feet, and lower back aches would touch every member of the team that season. Justin had endured intense training in high school but nothing like this, and certainly not into the season. He had endured two-a-day training for three weeks before each season began. Everyone used to refer to it as "hell month."

But once the three weeks were over, practices went to just once a day and eased up considerably. But Coach Moffit believed in only two types of practices, hard and harder. The two-a-days ended before the season began, but the intensity of the workouts never slowed. Justin often wondered if his body could hold up to the challenges of the workouts.

One thing was for sure, no one on the team had much time to get into trouble. Between the workouts, classes and studying, there just wasn't time or motivation. When the evenings and weekends came, rest and sleep seemed more inviting than the social events and parties outside the campus fences.

Ozark people loved to party, especially during the fall, winter and early spring when tourists weren't around, and there was very little else to do. Most restaurants and tourist activities closed after summer and didn't re-open until late spring. The sounds of traffic, people and outdoor activities were replaced with quiet. There wasn't much else to do but drink and party.

Many of those parties involved drugs. For that reason, the hosts were cautious. They held the parties in areas the police and strangers were less likely to find. Most were held in the woods, in open patches close to the lake. A favorite spot was on Outlook Mountain. It was called Outlook Mountain because it overlooked the tri-lakes that ran through the Branson area. It was the same mountain that Justin had run up many times in a weighted backpack during one of Coach Moffit's insane workouts. He had never been to the other side of the mountain, the side with a hidden gravel road that went up one side to the top where there was a reasonably flat area concealed on all four sides by trees. It was a perfect spot for a party.

The parties were secret, but somehow word of them always seemed to get around campus. There were always several students that found their way to the parties. Most of the time, they checked out of the dormitory for the weekend, saying they were going home when they instead partied the weekend away.

Earl Myers had attended many hill parties but not during cross-country season. He was dedicated, more so than anyone Justin had ever known. Earl gave 100% to everything he did. He had been a good influence on Justin. They were becoming very good friends even though they were nearly complete opposites.

Still, he considered Earl to be his best friend. Earl never pulled any punches. He said what he felt no matter what.

When it came to Risa, Earl was frank, "She's no good for you, buddy. I'm telling you, that girl is trouble. You're better off if you never see her again."

It bothered Justin when he said that, but he let it slide by.

Earl was too good of a friend to let his feeling for Risa change how he felt about him. Earl was different from any friend he had before. He was honest, and he would do anything for his friends. He was a big, clumsy guy with a heart ten sizes too big.

There were plenty of times that Earl's constant talking, his stupid practical jokes and his constant quoting of bible verses, drove Justin a little crazy, but still, he had never had such a strong friendship. He could tell Earl anything and know that he wouldn't be judged or that his conversations wouldn't be kept private. Justin told Earl about Elise, his first love.

"I loved her, Earl. I think that I still do. But we broke up when I left for S of O. She was afraid our relationship wouldn't work long-distance. She was going into her Senior year and wanted to date other boys. She wasn't ready to commit to just one guy. I understood, but it hurt. I miss her a lot."

"Why don't you write or call her?" Earl asked.

"I'm afraid that she might not answer. Besides, she's right. Our relationship couldn't have lasted. We are both too young to be in a serious relationship. It's better that we make a clean break."

"Well, buddy, there are plenty of cute girls right here on campus. Most of which, I think, would be anxious to date a city boy like you. You'd have it made here if you just opened yourself up to a good old hill girl. Trust me, hill girls know how to have fun. They also know how to cook and take care of their men, if you know what I mean. You could do a lot worse."

"Yeah, you are probably right, Earl, but I just don't think I'm ready yet. Besides, with the coach's insane workouts, all that I feel like doing when I get back to the dorm is sleeping."

"Hell, buddy, if you can sleep at night, you're not working out hard enough. The pains in my body keep me up most of the night."

"What about you, Earl? I don't see you dating any of the girls on campus."

"That's because it's cross-country season. That's my top priority now. Once the season is over, watch out, hill girls, because smooth Earl will be on the prowl. Justin, why did you decide to come to S of O. Don't misunderstand, but the school is a little out-of-character for a city boy like you."

"Well, to be honest with you, Earl, I sort of ran out of options. I had an illness my senior year that slowed my running. I lost my chance at a scholarship, and my parents couldn't afford to send me to college. Coach Moffitt thought he could get me back into shape, so when the school accepted me, I figured it was my best option. So, I came here."

"You could have walked on someplace else, maybe earned a scholarship after your first year."

"No, my parents couldn't afford to send me to college. They have enough trouble making ends meet. I did apply for financial aid at Kansas. But what they offered wasn't enough. Besides, it meant going into debt. I just didn't want to do that."

"What about you, Earl. Why did you choose S of O.?"

"I didn't consider anybody else, Justin. Hell, it really didn't matter to me whether I went to college or not. Nobody in my family ever went to college. I planned on getting a factory job, maybe in Springfield and building a small cabin on my family's property. But Coach Moffit called and asked me if I'd like to join his cross-country and track teams. School was free, and hell, I could always get a factory job if it didn't work out."

"Do you miss your family, Earl?"

"No, not really. My dad's an alcoholic. He stopped working several years ago, and now all he does is sit around the house and drink. He gets violent when he drinks. Mom and my younger brothers are afraid of him. But not me. He and I have tangled a few times. When he's drunk, I can whip his ass. To tell you the truth, I enjoy being away from home. Once in a while, I start missing mom and my brothers. When that happens, I can go home for a day or two. That's about as long as I can stand being home."

After the Rolla meet, S of O went up against Missouri

Southern in a dual meet in Joplin, MO. It was an unusually cold day for September, with temperatures in the fifties and the wind blowing gently out of the west. The race took place on Joplin's municipal golf course, a flat course conducive to achieving fast times. This was one of two races that season that Coach Moffitt specifically targeted to earn qualifying times at the NAIA National meet at the end of the season.

Most of the team figured that only one, maybe two of S of O's harriers had a shot at qualifying for Nationals. Brad Connelly had been to Nationals last year. He had been the only member of the team that year that did qualify, finishing 38th in a field of 180 runners.

Still, Brad had to qualify again this year, and his finishing time in the Rolla meet was nearly thirty seconds slower than the NAIA National qualifying time.

Coach Moffit also had hoped that Eric Cramer would qualify for Nationals also.

Ten minutes before the Joplin race was to begin, storm clouds moved overhead, and a light rain shower started. As the rain came down, the wind picked up too. When the starter's pistol went off, fourteen runners sprinted down a fifty-yard funnel-like start, with wide open space in the beginning and narrowing to a narrow pathway for most of the remainder of the course. Brad took the lead with Eric right on his shoulder. Justin and Earl, both known for their slow starts, were near the tail end of the pack. The first portion of the race went directly into the wind. Rain was intensifying and blowing almost horizontally directly into the runners' faces.

Justin settled in behind the backs of two Missouri Southern runners who shielded him from the wind and pounding rain. It was a strategy that would pay off for him. The first third of the race went straight west, right into the wind. But the second third of the race curled around the back portion of the golf course going northeast out of the direct impact of the wind. Justin was able to pass the two competitors directly in front of him when the running path widened slightly, and he no longer needed the bodies ahead of him to shield him from the wind and rain. He had conserved energy by staying behind the two runners during the windiest part of the run. Now he was preparing to make his move as he came out of the back of the course and began heading back to the finish.

That's when Earl's victory screams began. One after another as he passed competitors. Based on the number of screams, Justin reasoned, Earl must have been at the very back of the pack when he began his move.

The wind seemed to pick up as Justin turned back east for the final mile of the race. The blowing air seemed to lift him, pushing him faster than he thought he was capable of going. He was nearly at a full sprint when he passed the next two competitors. He counted only one Missouri Southern runner ahead of him as he reached the final, long, flat straightaway to the finish.

Earl's screams continued with every runner he passed. Justin could hear Earl's heavy breathing and loud footsteps directly behind him as he came up on the right shoulder of the top competitor. Fifty yards left. Justin, the Missouri Southern runner and Earl, were all in a full sprint to the finish line. They were side by side for the final twenty-five yards. Finally, Earl pulled ahead by a body length with Justin directly behind. All three runners crossed the finish line within one second of each other.

Coach Moffit had qualified four of his runners for the NAIA Nationals that day, more than any other season.

That night the team would celebrate in their suite on the fifth floor of the dormitory with pizza, cake and soda, compliments of Coach Moffit. He ordered pizza, and his wife Diane made the cake, three layers, chocolate cake with chocolate icing. Coach even rented the video *Hoosiers* to play on the common area television.

The party had barely begun when someone knocked on the door. It was a student.

"Is there a Justin in here?" he said.

"Yes, I'm Justin."

"There's someone downstairs to see you, a girl," the boy said with a grin.

"Who is it?" Justin asked.

"I don't know, man. She didn't give her name."

Justin excused himself and told his teammates that he would be right back. Then he went down the stairs to the first floor.

Waiting in the lobby was Risa. She smiled when she saw him.

"What are you doing here?" Justin asked.

It had been two weeks since he last saw her. She looked more beautiful than he remembered, but he refused to show his excitement to see her. She had not answered his calls. She simply vanished from his life with no explanation. He was hurt. He was angry with her.

"I came to see you, silly," she said with a wide grin.

"Where have you been for two weeks?" Justin asked.

"I've been here, just busy. I'm sorry we weren't able to talk. I've missed you."

"Well, you have a strange way of showing it. I tried calling you. I stopped by the dormitory. I even went to the bakery hoping to see you."

"Yeah, they transferred me out of the bakery. I'm working in the campus bookstore now. And, sorry about not returning your calls. Something happened, and I didn't feel that I should burden you. Can we take a walk and talk, Justin?"

"OK, but only for a few minutes. We're having a small pizza party upstairs. I told the team that I'd be right back."

She reached for Justin's hand. "I promise this will only take a few minutes. I just need to talk to you in private." She held his hand and led him out of the dormitory and down the concrete walkway toward the pond.

Her hand felt so warm, so tender, Justin thought. He wasn't going to admit it, but he missed her. She was like no other girl Justin had ever known. He was physically attracted to her, but it was much more than that. She seemed so genuine, so caring. There was a deep emotional connection between them. He couldn't explain it, but when he was with her, he was his happiest. He felt at peace.

The sky was clear, and the moon was full that night. The air was cool, with a slight breeze that was reminiscent of an early Fall evening. Risa wore a light blue sweater and tight blue jeans that framed her long, thin legs. Justin was under-dressed for the cool evening in shorts and a t-shirt. But the cool breeze felt good to him. He was just happy to be walking with Risa.

Clear, full-mooned nights on the S of O campus were a sight to be seen. Wide, cobblestone pathways that curled through campus leading from one building to another, all illuminated with old, iron post streetlights that looked like something from an old movie. And the bright, white lights of the fountain jetted water high in the air and arched back to the pond. With the white stone buildings serving as a backdrop, the campus looked like a set for a movie about college life many decades ago.

The ten-minute walk to the fountain was silent. Justin waited for Risa to talk, but she didn't. He could tell she had something heavy on her mind that she needed to tell him but was waiting for the right time and place to do so.

She led him to a bench on the far side of the fountain. It was quiet there. No other students were around, only the sound of the fountain in the background.

When seated, she reached over and gently kissed him on

the lips. It was a tender kiss, sweet, soft and long. She placed her hand on Justin's leg, looked him in the eyes and began to speak. "I'm so sorry if I hurt you, Justin. I didn't mean to. I care about you deeply. But there are things going on in my life that I wasn't able to share."

"OK, what's going on?" Justin asked.

"When I met you, there was an instant attraction. You are different from anyone that I have ever dated. I wanted to get to know you. I wanted our relationship to grow. The truth is that I had just broken up with someone. I thought it was over. I wanted it to be over. He's a boy that I knew from high school. We had dated for nearly four years. His family and mine are friends. They've known each other since I was born. Ever since we started dating, they assumed Richard and I would marry and settle down in Sikeston," Risa said with sad eyes.

"So where is this Richard now?" Justin asked.

"He's here at S of O. In fact, he lives at Brown Hall, on the third floor. He's a year older than me, a sophomore. He's a basketball player. You've probably seen him. He knows you."

"What?" Justin responded. "Did you tell him about us?"

"Yes, I had to. He forced me. You don't know Richard. He's a very jealous person. He has a dark side, a scary side. That's why I broke up with him, or at least, tried to break up with him. Richard doesn't take no for an answer. What he wants, he usually gets. You haven't been at S of O long enough to know that basketball players are treated like Gods on campus. The sport is hugely popular down here. But more than that, it brings in tons of revenue and keeps the alumni donating to the college. The entire third floor of Brown Hall is an athletic dorm for the basketball team. In addition, they have access to a lake home off campus, completely furnished by the alumni. That's where some of the team and alumni spend parts of the summer and weekends during the off-season. Team members can go there anytime they want. Richard is there tonight. That's why I felt safe talking to you, Justin."

"Are you afraid of him, Risa?"

"Not so much for me. I don't think that he would ever hurt me. But I am afraid for you. Like I said, Richard is a very jealous person, and he has a lot of friends. I told him that we only went out once and that it was over now. I think he believed me, but I'm sure he is keeping an eye on both of us."

"Risa, why did you want to talk to me tonight? Was it to warn me or tell me that we couldn't see each other again? Because I kind of assumed we were already over because you hadn't answered my calls or tried to see me the last couple of weeks."

"I wanted to see you, Justin. Richard had me stay with him at the lake house for the last two weeks. A friend of his saw us together coming back from our date. He told Richard, and Richard confronted me. He was so angry. I've never seen him that upset. He made me promise him that I would never see you again. That's when he made me pack my bags and move in with him at the lake house. Someone would drive me back for classes and pick me up afterward to go back to the lake house. I felt like a prisoner."

"How'd you get away tonight?"

"This weekend, the team is initiating the Freshman players. They're having a private party. None of the girlfriends are invited. He brought me back to campus late last night and will pick me up again tomorrow evening. He made me promise not to see you. Justin, I don't want to stop seeing you. I know that we don't know each other very well, but I feel there is something special about you. I feel so good when I'm around you. There is something special about the way I feel about you, and I think you feel the same way. Tell me you don't want to see me again, and I'll go away. But if you feel the same way about me that I feel about you, then we deserve to see how it works out."

Justin did feel the same way she did. His brain told him to walk away, but his heart wouldn't let him. He wrapped his arm around her, pulled her lips close to his and kissed her long and passionately. They spent the remainder of the evening before curfew in each other's arms on that bench on the other side of the fountain.

Risa was like no other woman Justin had ever known. She cast a spell on him that made it impossible for him to stop thinking of her.

The relationship is insane, he thought to himself. *Risa is dating another guy. She isn't willing to give Richard up. She wants to have him and me too. There is zero chance of our relationship ending well.*

Justin knew it was an unwinnable situation. He knew in his head that she would never leave Richard. She either loved him, or she was so afraid of him that she couldn't leave. Whatever the reason, Justin knew that the path he had decided to take would end in heartache. Still, in his heart, he couldn't walk away from her.

CHAPTER 4
LOVE GROWS

The next day was Sunday. Justin worked the early morning hours and then went to church with his teammates. Afterward, he picked up Risa at Claire Hall and drove to Springfield. It was about a forty-five minute drive from campus, enough time for them to talk, laugh, and forget about S of O for a little bit. They ate lunch at a small diner on the south side of town and then went to the mall to see a movie and do a little window shopping.

They talked about their families, their high school days, and what they wanted for their futures.

Risa wanted to become an artist or teach or maybe both. She promised to show Justin some of her work. Justin talked about coaching after graduating or writing for a large newspaper. He had been the sports editor of his high school paper and had also worked on the yearbook.

After the movie, they held hands and walked through the mall, talking and laughing.

"Can you ever see yourself living in a small town, Justin?" she asked.

"I don't know. I've only lived in the city before. Don't you get bored in a small town?" Justin asked.

"No, silly. There are plenty of things to do. Besides, if I did get bored, I'd just drive to the city. Take Sikeston, for instance.

We have movies, shopping, restaurants even a museum like the big cities, just on a smaller scale. Plus, you have the advantage of living at a slower, quieter pace. In Sikeston, we are always stopping to smell the roses. I think we enjoy life more because we're not so rushed."

"But, in the city, there are plenty of jobs. In Kansas City, we have professional Baseball and Hockey. No matter what kind of food you want, we have it. There's a zoo, large parks, museums, art galleries, theatre, concerts, nearly everything you can possibly want."

"Well, I'm not much into sports, and everything else is nice, but if I want it, I can always drive to Cape Girardeau or St. Louis. What about children, Justin? Have you thought about children?"

"No, not really. I guess that I want them someday."

"I want a big family, the bigger, the better, maybe three or four girls and a couple of boys."

"Geez, then you really should live in the city, Risa. You'll need a really good job to pay for all those kids."

"No, I can't see myself ever living in the city. I want to be close to my family. My parents, grandparents, uncles, aunts and most of my relatives live in Sikeston or close by. You should come to one of our Sunday dinners. Mom and Grandma make the best fried chicken, gravy, mashed potatoes, fresh corn on the cob with plenty of butter and homemade pies. Most of my relatives come over, and we spend the entire day together. Sometimes, they'll be twenty to thirty people in the house. It's crazy, but it's wonderful too. We're a very close family."

"I'd like to come over sometime. Our family isn't very large. We rarely have anyone over except for my grandparents."

When the mall closed at 6pm, Justin walked Risa to his car and opened the car door for her. Before she sat down, he gave her a long, tender kiss.

"My, what a gentleman you are, Justin. I believe that I could get used to this," Risa said.

On the way out of town, they stopped at McDonald's. It was what Risa wanted.

"I haven't had a good hamburger and fries in three months," she said.

"Then, why do you want to go to McDonald's?" Justin said jokingly.

"I think I'm addicted to their fries," Risa joked back.

"Let's get the food to go, Justin," Risa said. "I want to show you Rockaway Beach. We can eat our dinner at a picnic table there."

"OK, is it nearby?"

"It's on the way back to campus, just about fifteen minutes from here," she said.

Rockaway Beach was east of Highway 65, about halfway between Springfield and Branson. It was a small resort community with a picturesque lake nestled between two mountains. Rock ledges on one side of the lake were used by many of the local youth for diving. On the other side of the lake was a long, white sandy beach that was popular with tourists and perfect for swimming. It was a hidden paradise about five miles off the highway. During the summer months, tourists crowded the small, quaint town to shop and eat. The lake nearby and the beach were pleasant places to spend a hot summer day. But after Labor Day, the town was quiet, and the lake was typically used by locals for parties, skinny-dipping and romantic getaways.

It had a nice picnic area near the lake. Justin pulled into a small gravel parking lot near the beach area. They walked hand in hand to a picnic table close by, sat and ate their dinner.

"I think this is the most beautiful place in the Ozarks," Risa said. "Especially this time of year with the trees beginning to change. And this is the best time of the day to be here, just before sunset when the glow of the sun setting splashes across the lake with a rainbow of colors. Don't you think this is beautiful, Justin?"

He took a long look around the lake and focused his attention on the sun setting between two mountains to the west. "Yes, it's beautiful," he said. They held each other tight and kissed. At that moment, there was no place on earth where Justin would have rather been. "You are so beautiful, Risa," he said.

She lifted her head and looked directly into his eyes. She looked so relaxed, so content. "I think I could fall in love with you, Justin Wade."

It was nearly 9pm when they arrived back on campus.

"Shit," Risa said. "I forgot That Richard is picking me up. He's probably already here. Justin, I hate to ask you, but would you please drop me off at the front gate and then park. If he sees me with you, it's not going to be good, and I just don't want to confront him about you, not yet anyway."

Justin did what she wanted. She gave him a quick peck on the cheek. "I'll call you when I can," she said before climbing out of the car and walking briskly toward Claire Hall.

Justin didn't know what to think. This was the strangest relationship he had ever been in. His brain was telling him to forget about her, but his heart wouldn't let him. So, he parked the car and walked slowly back to Brown Hall. When he walked inside, he saw Risa waiting in the guest lobby. She was talking to another boy. Justin didn't recognize him. He thought about approaching her, but just as he started to, she gave him a quick glance and lowered her head. It was a look that told Justin not to come any closer. So, he walked away, went up the stairs and went back to his room. He was hurt, but mostly, he was confused. He cared deeply for Risa, more than he wanted to. There were lots of attractive women on campus that weren't already involved in a complicated relationship. Justin was handsome, athletic and could date a lot of women. But he wasn't interested in other women. He was only interested in Risa.

When Justin walked into the dorm room, the guys were sitting around in the living area watching television. It was about thirty minutes before lights out, and everyone was just trying to relax. They all turned around when Justin walked in, but no one said anything except Earl.

"Where have you been, Justin?" Earl asked when Justin walked into the dorm room.

"I was out with Risa. We went to Springfield today and just got back."

"Buddy, are you looking for trouble? That girl is dating Richard Conner. He's one of the captains of the basketball team and a jealous S.O.B. from what I hear."

"I know, Earl. There's just something about her that I can't help seeing her."

"Justin, trust me, there are plenty of women on campus that you can date that won't end up in getting your head split open. I know Richard. He's a big guy with a hell of a temper. Plus, he's got plenty of friends. He's not going to let you keep seeing his girlfriend without putting up a fight. Do yourself a favor. Stop seeing her."

"I wish I could, Earl, but I need to know how this plays out."

"OK, buddy. Just don't say that I didn't warn you."

"Hey, by the way, Justin. Coach came looking for you this afternoon."

"Why?"

"He didn't say. I told him you weren't here, and he said he would talk to you tomorrow."

"Justin, you should get some rest, and so should all of us," Brad Connelly said. "We've got a hard, resistance workout tomorrow afternoon, twelve miles and up and down Outlook Mountain with weight packs."

Brad was captain of the team, and he took his job seriously. Truth be told, he was a hell of a good leader. He kept the team in line. But the stare he gave Justin that night said he wasn't very happy with him. Brad wanted the team to stick together, especially during cross-country season.

"A team that sticks together wins together," he often said.

"There was no time for distractions and certainly no time for girls during the season," Brad had told the team just before the first summer practice.

Justin was breaking Brad's rules, and Brad's rules were Coach Moffit's rules. He wouldn't talk to Justin about it yet. But the look he gave him said it all.

On Monday, just before practice started, Coach Moffit called Justin into his office.

"Justin, the campus employment office has requested a new work assignment for you. They want you to become a bus driver for the athletic department. It seems that one of the drivers left campus unexpectantly, and they are short a driver. You, I understand, can drive a manual transmission and have a license that would allow you to drive buses. That, I'm told, is a valuable commodity around here. They have promised me that the bus driving won't begin until after cross-country season, so it won't interfere with your training. You are to report to Mr. Wilkinson after our season ends for your assignments."

"Yes, coach, is that all?"

"One last thing, Justin. I've been proud of you. You have shown a lot of promise. Your running has improved. When you first came to me after your sickness, asking for an opportunity, I must admit that I was a little hesitant. Your race times in high school were good but not great. The illness had set you back considerably, and there was no guarantee I could get you back into shape. And quite frankly, I was concerned that you would have a difficult time fitting in at S of O. You weren't used to the strict rules and the conservative environment we have here. Most city boys have difficulty here. But it seems that you have adjusted well."

"Thanks, coach."

"However, I am a little concerned about your relationship with a girl on campus. I understand that you are spending a lot of time with her. I also understand that she is dating another athlete at S of O. One thing that makes us such a close-knit community is that we don't shit in someone else's backyard. We have respect for our fellow athletes. Think of the athletes here as a big fraternity. We don't mess with our brothers, and we certainly don't try to take something away that belongs to them. Do you understand, Justin?"

"Yes, I think so, coach."

"In general, it's a good idea for my runners to stay away from girls all together until after the season. Your focus should be on God, running and studying. Why don't you do yourself a favor and forget about that girl."

"Is that all, coach?"

"Yes, why don't you finish getting ready for practice?"

The next three days were the toughest workouts yet. The team was moving from dual meet competitions to regional competitions. There would be many more runners and much stronger competition. S of O would be tested, and Coach Moffit wanted to ensure they were ready.

By Wednesday night, everyone was exhausted. Legs were numb with pain, feet were blistered, and the dormitory room reeked of Atomic Balm. The ointment brought relief but ate the hair off the legs and smelled like rotten eggs.

Coach Moffit believed in breaking the body down with intense workouts early in the week and then building it back up during the last few days before a race with long, slow runs that ended with laps in the campus indoor pool. The pool felt incredibly good after a long run, but Coach Moffit wasn't satisfied with just a dip or swim in the pool. He had to make it into a competition, running from side to side, lifting legs high and doing repetitions. The pool became an extension of the workouts. But the pool seemed to help aching joints and muscles. Legs weren't quite as tired at night, and with a little relief from the pain, sleeping became easier.

It was that Friday that posters began to appear all over campus. Devin Douglas, a junior at S of O, had disappeared. His parents and friends put up the missing student posters in nearly every building on campus. He was last seen a week earlier, leaving campus. There was no sign of him or the car he was driving.

"I knew Devin," Earl told Justin. "We had several classes together. He even drove the team to their meets last year. He was a bus driver, a good kid, kind of quiet, but a good kid. They say he just decided to quit school, packed his bags and left. Nobody has seen him since."

Justin had just returned from dinner that evening when he was stopped by a student at the front desk of Brown Hall.

"Hey, are you Justin Wade?" he asked.

"Yes, what do you want?"

"Someone left a note for you," he said, holding out an envelope addressed to Justin Wade.

"Thanks," Justin replied.

He put the envelope in his pants pocket and took it to his room. From the writing on the outside of the envelope, Justin had an idea who had written the note. But his teammates had come back with him after dinner, and he didn't want to open the letter in front of them.

When he got back inside the athletic suite, he excused himself to use the bathroom. Once inside, he opened the letter.

Justin,
I need to see you tonight. Can you sneak out after curfew, say

about midnight? I really need to talk to you, and I'm afraid we are being watched. The only time it is safe for us to meet is after the campus is locked down for the night. Please meet me at the bench by the fountain at midnight.

   Love,
   Risa

Every common sense instinct Justin had was to ignore that letter, to try to forget about Risa. She was trouble. He knew it.

Coach Moffit was right, he thought. *Don't shit in someone else's back yard.*

But his heart wouldn't let him do that. His emotions focused on the way she ended that letter, *"Love, Risa."* Was she falling in love with him? She had never spoken that word before.

Justin had strong feelings for her. He couldn't ignore them. He had to meet with her.

The team had a cross-country meet at Central Arkansas University in Conway, Arkansas, the next day. The bus would depart at 5am. It was going to be a short night. Coach had set a bedtime of 9pm that night. Everyone needed to be in bed at that time. He walked into the suite at 9:30pm to make sure everyone was in their rooms. He did that periodically to make sure that his rules were being followed. After he left, Justin lay in bed watching the clock. At 11:30pm, with everyone asleep, Justin climbed out the dormitory window and down the fire escape to the ground. He walked quietly amongst the shadows of the trees to the pond. Risa was already sitting on the bench when he arrived. She stood up and smiled when she saw Justin.

They hugged and kissed.

"I missed you so much, Justin," she said with a huge smile.

"I missed you too, Risa," he said back.

"What's going on, Risa? Your letter worried me. You sounded afraid."

"I am. Richard has people watching both of us. I told him we have stopped seeing each other, but he doesn't believe me. I think they are planning something for you. Justin, you need to be careful. Richard's even more jealous than I thought he was. He hates you, and so do his friends. I wouldn't blame you if you never wanted to see me again. I've caused you a lot of trouble."

"What about you, Risa? Are you afraid that he might hurt you?"

"No, I don't think he would do that. He's angry with me, but I don't think he would hurt me. Inside, he is really a gentle soul. But it's his silly pride that gets in the way. He thinks because we have dated so long, that I belong to him. He has always figured that we would marry after both of us graduate. Now, he sees you interfering with those plans. He sees you as the problem, and his friends see you as an outsider trying to destroy the relationship that Richard and I have had. If someone comes after you, I don't think it will be Richard. I think it will be his friends."

"Risa, do you love him?"

Risa lowered her head. A tear rolled slowly down her cheek. "I don't know. I care about him a lot, and if you had asked me if I loved Richard before I met you, I would have said 'yes.' But now I'm confused. I have strong feelings for you, Justin, feelings that I haven't had for Richard in a long time."

Risa raised her head, wiped the teardrop from her face and smiled at Justin. "I think I'm falling in love with you, Justin."

He put his arm around her, pulled her close to him, and they kissed.

Justin had never felt like this about anyone before. His heart ached for her. She was so beautiful. There was no place he would rather be than where he was that very moment, holding her tight and feeling the warmth and tenderness of her body.

He took her hand, lifted her gently from the bench and walked her to an open part of grass between the shadows of the trees and the light of the fountain. He took off his shirt and laid it on the ground. He looked into her eyes. The light from the fountain seemed to radiate from her blue eyes, giving them a softness he had never seen before. He looked into her face. She smiled tenderly.

They kissed long and soft. Then again, with passion. He lifted her blouse slowly at first, waiting for any sign of objection. There was none. He gazed at her pink, lacey bra, which gave him the slightest hint of what was underneath. He tried to remove her bra, but his hands were shaking. She put her hand on his arm, gently pulling it away. She held his hand for an instant and then moved her hand to the latches on the back of her bra, undoing them and allowed her bra to slide down to the ground.

"Don't be nervous," she said to him. "It's OK. I want you to make love to me."

God, she is the most beautiful woman I've ever seen, he thought.

He lifted his shaking hand to her breasts, gently rubbing his hand around them while kissing her with a passion he had never felt before. He lifted her up and laid her down on the ground. She opened her arms to his. The light of the fountain shined on their naked bodies as they made tender, sweet love.

It was that night that Justin knew that he was in love. It was the night that would change his life forever.

CHAPTER 5
A DANGEROUS TIME

Justin got no sleep that night. By the time he got back to the dorm, it was nearly time to wake up to catch the bus for the cross-country race at Central Arkansas University. He would need to get his sleep on the bus. His teammates were still asleep when he entered the room through the rear window.

That is good, he thought. *No one will notice I've left.*

He walked quietly into his room, put on his pajamas on and got into bed. Earl was snoring loudly in the other bed. That was a sure sign that he was sound asleep. Justin had gotten used to his snoring. He rarely noticed it anymore. At that moment, it was welcomed. He didn't want anyone to know that he had been out of the room that night, and he certainly didn't want anyone to know that he was with Risa.

He laid in bed for only a few minutes when the alarm clock went off. It was still dark outside. The bus would be leaving in thirty minutes. There was only enough time to get the uniforms, pack a small bag for a change of clothes after the race and get to the bus. When the team traveled a long distance for a race, Coach Moffit required everyone to bring a suit and tie to change into after the race. He wanted his team to look sharp when they went to dinner together after the race, even if that dinner was a meal at McDonald's.

Coach Moffit wore a suit and tie to every race. At first,

Justin thought his coach looked silly wearing a suit on the cross-country course when all the other coaches wore shorts or sweatpants and tee shirts. He looked particularly silly wearing tennis shoes with his suit.

But Earl put everything into perspective. "Coach is set in his ways. He's not going to change, and that's a good thing. He is the most honest, genuine person you will ever meet. There is nothing he cares more about than the team, and he wants others to respect them as much as he does. The suits are one way he shows others that S of O is no ordinary college and his athletes are special young men."

Justin had gained a great deal of respect for Coach Moffit during the last several weeks. There were times he hated his coach for how hard he pushed the team and for the rules he demanded the team follow. But there were even more times that he respected and admired Coach Moffit. He was usually right, and no one could fault his motives. He cared deeply for every athlete on the team. His only objective was to make them better athletes and better men.

It was exactly 4am when the bus pulled out of the parking lot. It was a 4-hour ride to Conway, Arkansas, where the race would take place at 10am. Coach's wife had made breakfast for the team, homemade cinnamon rolls, egg and bacon burritos, orange juice and coffee. They ate on the bus. After breakfast, most of the team laid back and took a nap. Brad Connelly and Earl Myers were the exceptions. They were wide awake. Earl was energized after eating three cinnamon rolls and downing them with four cups of black coffee. Brad took one for the team by allowing Earl to bounce his wild ideas and silly conspiracy theories off him so the others could rest.

"You know Brad. No one has actually walked on the moon. In fact, no one has even landed on the moon. Neil Armstrong took those famous steps in the New Mexico desert. It was all staged for the public," he said to Brad. "And, do you know that the CIA had JFK assassinated. They were upset about Cuba. Kennedy wouldn't allow them to invade Cuba, and that's why they assassinated him. They wanted to take over Cuba and use it as a secret base."

Brad listened to every crazy thing Earl had to say, nodding his head when Earl looked at him, waiting for acknowledgement that he was listening.

Tyler had just crossed the Arkansas border heading south on Highway 65, when the rain started, slow at first and then heavy. The mountain roads were steep and slick. Visibility was poor. Tyler slowed the bus down the hills and increased power going back up the hills. About sixty miles north of Conway, the brakes gave out on a long downhill stretch of the highway. It gained speed as it descended. The drop-offs on either side of the road were huge. Tyler pumped the brakes over and over again. They were useless. He shifted the gear into neutral to try to slow down. It didn't help. His hands gripped the steering wheel, trying to keep the bus on the road. Three times he hit the guard rail on the side of the road. By the third bump of the guard rail, everyone on the bus was wide awake.

"Hang on," Trevor yelled. "I don't think I can keep the bus on the road."

At the bottom of the hill, the bus was traveling seventy miles an hour. Trevor had managed to keep the bus on the road until he reached an uphill section of the highway. The bus slowed to forty miles per hour near the top of the uphill. That was when Trevor saw a relatively flat portion of land on one side of the highway. He decided to go off the road to get the bus to stop rather than chance going down another hill. His decision paid off. The bus went another sixty feet off the road and stopped when it hit a large oak tree.

Everyone on the bus was shaken. Bobby Cockran banged

his head against a window, cracking the window and causing him to pass out for a short time. Dennis Glenn received a deep cut just below his right knee, and Justin twisted his ankle and banged the arch of his left foot.

Coach Moffit used his cell phone to call for help. It was nearly thirty minutes before help arrived. Bobby Cockran and Dennis Glenn were taken to the Conway Hospital to be treated. Neither of their injuries was serious.

Justin wrapped his ankle tightly and was able to walk. The deep bruise to his arch was a little more serious than his ankle, although he didn't realize it at the time.

Just after the ambulance left, a bus from Central Arkansas University arrived to take the team to Conway.

"Coach Moffit?" the bus driver asked. "Coach Wallace wants to know if your team still wants to race. If they do, Coach said he'll hold up the race until you get there and have plenty of time to warm up."

Coach Moffit turned to his team. "It's up to you guys. We only have five runners. Do you guys still want to race today?"

Brad Connelly spoke for the team. "Yes, absolutely. It will take more than a little accident to stop S of O."

"OK, then," Coach Moffit said. "Tell Coach Wallace that we want to run."

The team arrived at Central Missouri University an hour later, shaken but determined to compete. Justin put atomic balm on his twisted ankle, wrapped it as tightly as he could and began to warm up. Every step he took on the injured ankle was painful, but he had to run. With two of his teammates unable to compete, Justin was the fifth runner. The team had to have five runners finish the race in order not to be disqualified.

When the starter's gun went off, twenty-six runners from four schools took off down a long straightaway that funneled into a narrow path a quarter mile into the race. Justin hobbled to the rear of the pack and was sitting in third to last place when the pathway narrowed. His ankle throbbed with pain but what was worse was the bruised arch on his left foot. Every step he took felt like a knife jabbing into his foot.

Justin tried several times to speed up, to pass runners and make a move in the pack. But, the pain in his foot and ankle were too intense. Halfway through the race, he resigned himself to just finishing the race. During the final straightaway to the finish, he was unable to sprint and was passed by the only two runners that were behind him.

For the first time ever, Justin finished in last place. He wasn't the only one that struggled. The bus accident had shaken everyone. S of O finished in last place as a team.

S of O sent another bus down to pick up the team. Bobby Cochran and Dennis Glenn were released from the hospital and joined the rest of the team for the bus ride home. The team was quiet on the ride home. It was a depressing day, and it provided everyone a reality check of how quickly a team can go from winners to losers.

For days, the bus accident was the talk around campus. Most people assumed that the brakes on the bus gave out from a combination of the rain and mountainous roads. Some blamed Trevor.

"He was driving too fast for the conditions," Justin heard one student say. "He was too inexperienced for those mountain roads," another said.

There was even a rumor going around campus that the brake lines had been cut and that someone was trying to kill Trevor or a member of the team.

For all the speculation, there was one curious thing that happened after the accident. Trevor dropped out of school immediately after the bus accident. He didn't talk to anyone. He simply packed his bags when he got back to campus and left.

Risa had moved back to the condo in Branson on the day of the accident. Justin found a note that she had left for him when he got back from Arkansas. The note was given to a student who slid it under Justin's dorm room door.

Justin,
Last night was wonderful. I will cherish it forever. You are in my dreams and in my heart. But we must not see each other for a while. Richard suspects that we have been seeing each other. He is very upset. I need to move off campus for a while. We shouldn't see each other until it is safe. I'll write you whenever I can.
Love,
Risa

The letter was signed with her lips pressed against the paper creating an image of a kiss in red lipstick.

Justin had never been in love before. But he was afraid he was now. He didn't want to be, certainly not with someone that was in another relationship. His head told him to never see her again, to let her go. But his heart wouldn't let that happen. He would be patient, wait for her, and let her relationship with Richard run its course.

Justin believed in his heart that soon Risa would realize that Richard was too controlling, that he wasn't the right person for her.

That's when she will break the relationship off with him and come back to me, he thought. *That's when she will come back to me for good.*

Women had always been difficult for Justin to figure out. But Risa was more confusing than any woman he had known before. She said she loved him, but she also seemed to love Richard. She appeared to be a very strong-willed woman but yet she let Richard control her. She didn't seem content in her relationship with Richard, but she was unwilling to break up with him. Justin had no idea where he stood with her.

The extent of Justin's injury to his foot became apparent during his workout Monday. Coach Moffitt called for a long slow run, twelve miles at a comfortable pace. Justin took off with the team but had to stop less than a mile into the run. Pains shot up from his foot to his ankle, so intense that he had to stop his run and walk back to campus.

Coach Moffitt was waiting for him when he got back.

"You're going to need to get that foot checked out. I want you to go to Dr. Barrow in Branson tomorrow after classes. He's a Podiatrist that has helped our team in the past. He'll let us know what needs to be done to heal your foot bruise," Coach Moffitt said.

"OK, coach. I'll go see him tomorrow."

The mood that night in the dorm room was somber. The team had seen their first defeat over the weekend. Bobby Cochran and Dennis Glenn were still hobbled from their injuries in the bus accident, and now it looked like Justin might be out for a while. A season that looked so promising just a week earlier was now in jeopardy of falling apart.

Brad Connelly, who was always optimistic, had nothing to say. Earl Myers, the most talkative member of the team, sat quietly on the couch, sipping a glass of water and watching television, no jokes, no words of wisdom, none of his silly conspiracy theories. No one was in the mood to talk.

X-rays taken at Dr. Barrow's office the next day confirmed Justin's fear. He had a deep bruise to the arch of his foot. The only solution to healing it was rest, six to eight weeks, maybe longer. Justin would need to stay off of his foot as much as possible. His season was over.

Immediately after Dr. Barrow gave Justin the bad news, he called Coach Moffitt.

The coach came to see Justin and talk to the rest of the

team that night at Brown Hall.

"I'm sorry, Justin. It looks like you're going to miss the rest of the season. I want you to rest that foot whenever you can. Use the hot tub in the athletic building every day after classes, ice your foot up at night and wrap it every day. Don't walk on it unwrapped.

"Gentlemen, I don't need to tell you how challenging the remainder of the season is going to be. We have only six healthy runners, and we're facing stiffer competition every week. Daryl, Dennis and Bobby, we need each of you to work as hard as possible to fill those fourth and fifth positions. Those positions are going to make or break our team scores for the remainder of the season. Brad, Eric and Earl, you need to lead the others in practices and in the remainder of our meets. Push yourself and push the others. We've got a strong team. Justin's injury is just a bump in the road. If everyone else stays healthy and we keep our minds strong and our bodies even stronger, we can still have an outstanding season."

"Justin, your work assignment has been changed to something that I believe will give your foot the best chance of healing, so you'll be fresh and ready for the track season next semester. I need you to report to Karl Gholson, the athletic director, tomorrow at 4pm. He will give you your assignment."

"Yes, coach."

The next day, Justin walked to his Economics class just after breakfast. On the pathway, he spotted Risa walking in the opposite direction.

"Risa," he hollered.

She ignored him. He was certain she heard him. Her eyes looked at him for a split second, then lowered to the walkway.

Damn, he thought. *Is she afraid someone is watching her*? He didn't know. But whatever was going on, he didn't understand.

At 4pm, Justin knocked on Karl Gholson's door. "Come

in," he said.

Justin stepped inside. "Mr. Gholson, I'm Justin Wade. Coach Moffitt told me to report to you for a new work assignment."

"Oh, yes, Mr. Wade. I understand you have a class B driver's license."

"Yes, sir."

"We need another bus driver for our athletic teams. As you can imagine, finding students who can drive our buses and have the proper license is not easy. We'd like to get you started right away. I'll post the assignments every week outside my office. The keys and bus assignments are in our transportation building on the southeast edge of campus. The job requires that you be flexible. If an assignment interferes with your class schedule, you will receive an excused absence. You will find that the job has several perks, including extra pay that is above and beyond what goes toward your tuition. Do you have any questions, Mr. Wade?"

"When will I start?"

"Right away. Your first assignment will be posted tomorrow."

Justin was assigned to drive the bus for the cross-country team for the remainder of the season. It was what he had hoped for. He could be with the team, watch their races and drive the bus that got them there and brought them home.

He admitted to Earl that he had mixed feelings about driving the team, though. "It will be great to be with you guys, to be able to watch the races. But it's going to be sad not to be able to compete."

"Hey, buddy, at least you'll be with us. All the guys will be glad you'll be there to support them. I just hope you drive that bus better than Tyler, but from the way I've seen you drive your car, I'm not so sure."

"Very funny, Earl."

"Hey, I forgot to mention Justin. Somebody left a letter for you. It was under our door when I came back from classes today," Earl said, handing him a plain white, sealed envelope that was addressed to Justin.

He took it and opened the envelope. It was a letter from Risa.

Dear Justin,

I saw you on the way from class today. I wanted to talk to you, but one of Richard's friends was just a few steps behind me. I hope you understand. I just can't do anything to upset Richard. I was sick when I heard about your bus accident. I tried to find out as much as I could about what happened, but all I got were the rumors floating around campus. They said two of your teammates were in the hospital. Then someone said you were injured too. My heart dropped when I heard that. Brad Connelly is in one of my classes. I asked him about you. He said you had a bruised foot and would not be able to run for the remainder of the season. I'm so sorry, Justin. I wish I could be with you, hold your hand and tell you how much I love you. Someday, we'll be together and laugh about this ridiculous situation. I know it's hard for you to understand, but I really do want to be with you. I can't leave Richard right now. But there will come a time soon when we will be together. Please be patient with me.

Love,
Risa.

Justin folded up the letter and put it in his pocket.

"Who wrote you, buddy?" Earl asked.

"Risa," Justin answered.

"Damn, buddy. I thought you had given up on her. She's trouble. More specifically, her boyfriend and his friends are trouble."

"I know, Earl. I wish I could just walk away, but I can't."

"Okay, buddy. You know if they come after you, I'll be

there to back you up."

"I know, Earl. Thanks."

The team's next race was Saturday in St. Louis. It was an invitational event set up by the host school, Washington University. There would be ten teams, all larger schools from the Midwest, racing in Forest Park, a sprawling park in the central west end of St. Louis. Justin's instructions were to pick the bus up at 4:00am, drive it to the athletic building, pick up the team at 4:30am and begin the four-and-a-half-hour journey to Forest Park.

He was sound asleep at 3:30am when the alarm went off. He dressed quickly and hurried out of Brown Hall fifteen minutes later. The bus lot was a ten-minute walk from the dormitory. It was completely dark outside, except for a nearly full moon peeping through dense clouds. It had been raining just a few minutes earlier. The air was moist and cool. There was a thin layer of fog that had crept up from the lakes below in the valley. The cool weather chilled Justin's bones but helped him wake up during his short walk. He hadn't had a chance to grab a cup of coffee before he left Brown Hall. He hoped the office where the bus keys and sign-out sheets were located had a pot of coffee going. He didn't particularly like the taste of coffee, but he desperately needed the caffeine it provided. *If there isn't a pot of coffee there*, he thought, *Coach will have a thermos of it when he gets on the bus. I can get a cup or two from him.*

Coach Moffitt hated the early morning trips. It took him several cups of strong, black coffee before anyone could talk to him without him biting their heads off.

The lights from the fountain illuminated the first five minutes of Justin's walk. After that, he had nothing more than a glimmer of moonlight to guide his way to the bus lot. It was eerily quiet that early in the morning. All he could hear were his footsteps moving across the gravel roads leading to the parking lot. When he arrived at the lot, he walked into the building where his keys would be waiting. The building was a small steel structure, no more than fifteen feet long by twenty feet wide. Inside, the lights were on, and a young man, a student, it appeared, was seated behind a small, wooden desk.

"Hello, you must be Justin," the student said with a stoic look on his face.

"Yes, who are you?"

"I'm Richard Conner, Risa's boyfriend. It's about time that we meet."

CHAPTER 6
AN UNWANTED JOB

"Oh, shit, what do you want?" Justin said.

"I'm your boss, asshole," he said, glaring back at Justin. "You and I have some personal issues that need to be settled. But that's not going to happen now. We'll talk about that some other time. I need to clue you in on your job right now."

"Ok, Richard."

"First, I want you to know that it wasn't my idea to have you drive busses. I don't want anyone working here that I can't trust, and I sure as hell can't trust you. You have certain skills that got you this job. I've got to live with that, but I don't need to like it, and I plan to make your time here as difficult as possible. Do you understand?"

"Yes."

"If I have anything to do with it, you're going to get the crappiest busses and the worst assignments. I hope for both our sakes that you quit, maybe even drop out of school. But until then, I need to make sure you abide by the rules. Mr. Gholson probably told you about the opportunities to earn extra income. But I'm sure he didn't provide you any details of what you need to do to earn that income.

"Justin, on certain trips, a backpack with your name on it will be loaded into your bus, which must not be opened or removed until someone contacts you when you reach your destination. When you are carrying this backpack, you are not to leave the bus for any reason. When you reach your destination, do not let any of the team members remove it. It will be labeled with your name on it. It must remain on the bus until someone approaches you with an S of O business card and mentions my name. When they do, you are to hand them the backpack, and they will hand you an identical backpack with your name on it. You are not to leave the bus. You are not to leave that bag unattended. You are not to open either backpack. They are sealed, and we will know if they have been opened. You will deliver the backpack left with you back to me at this office when you return to campus. I will pay you a cash bonus for every successful trip."

"What the hell are you up to, Richard?" Justin asked.

"Don't question it, asshole. It's none of your business and trust me when I say that if you tell anyone about our arrangement, you're going to find yourself floating at the bottom of the campus pond. Justin, I'm telling you that this is something you don't want to ask questions about. The less you know, the better. Just do exactly as I tell you, and you'll make good money and live to spend it."

It was at that point that Justin realized that Richard knew and perhaps even had something to do with the two bodies in S of O's fountain.

Richard continued. "You happen to be traveling with a special backpack today. Make sure it is safely transferred to St. Louis, and make damn sure that the backpack given to you in the exchange is returned to me. If you fuck this up, asshole, you won't live to see tomorrow. If you think about crossing me or telling someone about our conversation, consider that I am not the only one that knows about our arrangement, and if you screw me over, you're also screwing people that are a hell of a lot meaner than me. They wouldn't stop at killing you. They will go after your family and anyone close to you. And, if you're thinking of quitting this job, or walking away, understand that no one walks away without serious consequences."

Richard handed him the keys to bus 13. "You may recognize the bus you'll be driving today. It's the same one that Tyler drove last weekend when the brakes went out, and he crashed it into a tree," Richard said with a smile. "Don't worry, though. I'm pretty sure the brakes have been fixed. Funny thing about Tyler, he didn't much like the arrangement we had, but he managed to keep his mouth shut. I trust you'll do the same."

Five minutes later, Justin was on the bus and pulling up to the athletic building. Coach Moffitt was waiting. "Justin, I'm glad you're driving us. I hope you're a better driver than Tyler. We don't need any more accidents."

"Yes, coach. I agree. Do you think I could have a cup of coffee from your thermos before we take off?"

"Sure, get the bags loaded, and I'll pour you a cup. Hope you like it black and strong."

"Absolutely, the stronger, the better."

The team was arriving now. As they did, they left the bags at the rear of the bus for loading. He opened the luggage compartment at the bus's rear to start loading. That's when he noticed the black backpack already loaded inside. It had a tag on it marked "Justin Wade." It looked like a plain, ordinary backpack. There was nothing suspicious about it. He loaded the team bags in front of it, shut the compartment and got on the bus.

"Hey, Justin," Earl hollered. "Have you ever driven a bus before?"

"No, but there's a first for everything," Justin said, smiling back at his friend.

"I just hope Tyler didn't give you lessons," Earl replied.

Then Eric spoke up. "Justin, isn't this the same bus that we wrecked last week. It still has a dent in the front where it struck that tree."

"Yeah, it's the same bus. But they assured me that the brakes have been fixed."

"Well, I hope you tested them before you came to pick us up," Earl said, laughing.

"No, I didn't have time. I thought we'd test them together on the hills going up to Springfield."

"Very funny, Justin," Earl replied.

The buses in S of O's fleet consisted mainly of retired school buses, repainted and refurbished by student mechanics. Most were ten years old or older. The one Justin was driving was closer to fifteen years old. The floor was rusting. The seats were torn. Several of the windows were cracked, and others wouldn't open. The heater barely worked. The cross-country team was used to getting some of the worst busses. There were some new ones in the campus fleet, but those were used for the basketball and baseball teams. Those were the two sports that brought in the most revenue and alumni support to S of O.

The basketball team had been to the NAIA tournament for six of the last ten years. They had won regionals the last two years. Stands were packed for their games, and they even had local television and radio contracts. The baseball team had even more success than the basketball team, although they brought in less than half the revenue. They had been runners-up to the NAIA National Championship twice and had won Regionals four of the last six years.

Other sports teams at S of O were treated like bastard children compared to the basketball and baseball teams. Their budgets were smaller for equipment, uniforms and travel expenses. They rarely attended competitions that were too far for the team to be able to drive to and back from on the same day. Baseball and Basketball teams got the priority on the athletic building's facilities like the weight room, locker rooms, hot tub and swimming pool.

In reality, S of O wasn't much different than most private schools whose resources were limited and who prioritized budgets based on projected revenue to the athletic department.

Based on income-producing ability, the cross-country team was at the bottom of the list. They brought in zero income, and their travel expenses were high. Coach Moffitt had done the best he could with his limited resources. His teams had done well, and the cross-country program at S of O was highly regarded. He had a reasonable amount of pull with the school's administrators, and he used that pull whenever he felt it was necessary. He had used that pull to get approval to travel to larger competitions like the one they were going to that day in St. Louis. He had also used that pull to get the team into a special athletic dorm suite at Brown Hall. Other than the Basketball and Baseball teams, no other teams roomed together in Brown Hall.

The trip to St. Louis was long but uneventful. Most of the team slept. Justin spent his time thinking about Richard and that backpack.

What was inside it?

Who was the person that was going to pick it up?

What was Richard involved in, and did Risa know anything about it?

Did Richard kill the boys in the pond, and why were they killed? Did it have something to do with what was in that backpack?

Who were the others involved that Richard alluded to? Was Karl Gholson involved? Was Coach Moffitt involved?

Tyler was involved, according to Richard.

Did his involvement have anything to do with the bus accident? Is that why he left school so abruptly?

At this point, Justin had no answers. All he had were questions. He wanted to tell someone. Whatever Richard was up to had to be illegal.

But what if Richard's threats are true? What if other people were involved, people that would not think twice about harming me or my family?

He couldn't take that chance, not yet, not until he had more answers, not until he knew exactly what Richard was up to and who else was involved.

Forest Park was nestled in the central west end of St. Louis. It was bordered on the north and west side by million-dollar homes and mansions built in the early to mid-1900s. On the east side were elegant restaurants and Barnes Jewish Hospital. On the south side was Highway 40, a major highway connecting downtown to the east and the suburbs to the west.

The race was to begin in the northern section of the park between the art and history museums and the public golf course. Justin parked the bus in a public parking lot across from the golf course. He opened the door and wished each team member good luck as they got off the bus.

"Aren't you coming, buddy?" Earl asked.

"No, I can't. I was given instructions not to leave the bus."

"Nobody is going to know, Justin," Earl said. Come on, you can see the start and finish of the race from the terrace of the golf course."

"No, this is my first day driving. I better follow the rules."

"What? Are they afraid someone might steal this old bus? They'd be doing us all a favor if they did steal it," Earl said jokingly.

"Good luck, Earl. Do me a favor and shout as loud as you can so I can hear you every time you pass someone."

"I'll do that, buddy. See you on the other side."

Justin waited anxiously for about thirty minutes before someone approached the bus. He was a young man with stringy, long hair with tattoos covering his arms and legs. He looked a bit like a homeless person. His clothes were dirty and worn. He was smoking a cigarette.

He knocked on the door of the bus. At first, Justin was afraid to let him in. Then, he pulled out a business card with School of the Ozarks printed in large letters. Justin opened the door to the bus.

"What the fuck, man?" he said. "I thought you weren't going to let me in. Got the backpack for me?"

"Yes, it's in the back. Do you have something for me?"

"First things first, asshole. You give me your backpack, and I'll give you mine."

Justin went to the back of the bus and got the backpack. He handed it to him. Without saying a word, the man took the backpack and started to walk away.

"Hey, wait. You're supposed to give me one."

"Be patient, little man. I've got to make sure you're giving me everything. I'll be back."

Justin watched the man disappear behind several rows of cars. He was gone about ten minutes before he returned carrying another backpack. He said nothing, just threw the backpack inside the bus and left.

Justin was shaking. Everything about the man gave him the creeps. He took the backpack and stuffed it underneath his driver's seat. All he wanted to do was to get the hell out of there. But he had to wait for the team.

"How'd you guys do?" he asked as the team returned to the bus.

"We finished sixth," Brad Connelly said back.

From the looks on the other runner's faces, it was going to be a long, quiet ride home. That was fine with Justin. He wasn't in the mood for conversation. His mind could not get away from that backpack and what kind of trouble he was involved in. He worried about Risa.

Does she know about Richard?" he wondered. *"Is that why she is afraid to leave him?*

One thing was certain, he needed to talk to her as soon as possible.

It was a little past 8pm when Justin arrived back on campus. He dropped his teammates off and drove the bus to the parking lot. He grabbed the backpack and walked to the office. Lights were on inside. Seated at the desk was Richard.

"Let's have the bag, asshole," he said as Justin entered the office.

Justin handed him the bag and watched as he examined the outside to make sure the lock was not tampered with and the bag hadn't been opened. Then he reached into the desk drawer and pulled out an envelope. He sat it on the edge of his desk.

"Take it. You earned it," he said to Justin.

"I don't want it," Justin responded.

"Take it, damn it," Richard said. "If you don't, someone might get the idea that you aren't to be trusted, and I don't think you want them to think that. Although, if you don't take it, I believe I will enjoy watching them deal with you."

Justin reached down to take the envelope. Richard grabbed his arm before he could lift it from the desk.

"Just one more thing, asshole. Stay away from Risa. Someone else may think you are useful, but I swear to you, if you continue to see Risa, I'll fucking kill you."

Richard released Justin's arm and let him pick up the envelope.

Justin took the envelope, put it in his pants pocket and walked out the door without saying anything.

He walked back toward Brown Hall, stopping at the bench on the far side of the fountain first. It was a chilly night, temperatures in the forties with a slight breeze that made it feel ten degrees cooler. The area was quiet. No one was around. He sat on the bench, pulled out the envelope and opened it. Inside were ten twenty-dollar bills.

Justin suspected that what he delivered to St. Louis was illegal. Now he was certain of it.

Whatever Richard had involved him in was bad. He knew that. He sat on the bench wondering what he could do, wondering who he could trust, wondering if Risa was involved. He sat on that bench for over an hour thinking. Then he walked to Brown Hall and to his room.

"Where have you been, buddy?" Earl asked. "We've been back for over an hour."

"Just needed to clear my head," Justin replied.

"Well, sit down. Have a beer," Bobby said, holding out a cold Budweiser. "Earl and I went into town and bought a case. We figured the team needed to relax and unwind after the terrible day we had."

"Thanks, Bobby. I didn't realize either of you were twenty-one," Justin said.

Both Bobby and Earl laughed.

"We're not," Bobby said, "but Earl has a driver's license that says he is."

"How'd you manage that, Earl?" Justin asked.

"Twenty bucks and a name of a senior that is a whiz making fake IDs," Earl replied.

Justin looked around. Besides Earl and Bobby, Dennis Glenn was the only other teammate in the common living area of the suite.

"Where are the others?" Justin asked.

"They went to their rooms," Earl said. "They were afraid coach might stop by, and they didn't want to get him any madder than he already was."

Bobby held out his beer. "Let's toast to better days, boys."

Everyone tapped beers and then took swallows.

"Man, this beer tastes good," Justin said.

"Damn right," Earl said.

"By the way, where were you, Justin?" Bobby asked.

"I needed to walk and think a little bit. It was a stressful day."

"Stressful? all you did was drive the bus. We're the ones that had our asses kicked and then had to listen to coach scream at us," Dennis said.

"OK, enough talk about today's race," Bobby said. "Let's talk about something pleasant."

"Like girls?" Dennis said.

"I think you better talk about a subject you know something about, Dennis," Earl said, laughing.

"Buddy, I saw Risa tonight outside the liquor store in Branson," Earl said. "She was waiting in a car, a new red Camaro. She was on the passenger side with the window rolled down. She called me over when she saw me. She asked about you, Justin, and how you were doing. I told her that you were doing OK. Then she saw someone coming out of the liquor store and motioned me away. She looked afraid."

"Did you see who the guy was?"

"Yeah, I saw him, but I didn't recognize him. I don't think he was one of Richard's teammates or another S of O student, though. He was short and heavy-set with long thin hair tied into a ponytail. He had tattoos all over. I tell you, he looked a little scary to me."

"Damn, Earl. Do you think she is in some kind of trouble?"

"I don't know, buddy. But I think if she was worried that she would have said something to me, asked for help or told me to call the police."

"You really seem to care about that girl," Bobby said.

"Yes, I do," Justin replied. "I'm worried about her. I think she may be mixed up with some bad people."

"Why do you say that?" Dennis asked.

Justin grabbed another beer, opened it and drank it down

quickly. He needed a little liquid courage for what he was about to tell them.

After downing the beer, he put the empty can on the coffee table and stood up.

"Boys, if I tell you something, can you promise not to tell anyone? I mean, absolutely no one else can know."

They all agreed.

Justin pulled the envelope from his pocket, opened it and set the $200 that was inside it on the table.

"Damn, buddy. Where did you get that much money?" Earl asked.

"I got it from Richard Conner, Risa's boyfriend," Justin said.

"Oh shit," Earl responded. "What's going on? Did he try to pay you off to stop seeing Risa?"

"No. He wants me to stop seeing Risa, alright. He even threatened to kill me. But that wasn't what the money was for," Justin said.

That's when he told his friends the whole story. They sat there and listened to every detail. When Justin was done with his story, Bobby was the first one to speak up.

"It's got to be drugs," he said. "Drugs are big in the Ozarks, marijuana, cocaine, meth. They're all being produced down here."

"How do you know that?" Dennis asked.

"Remember, I grew up in the hills of the Ozarks. Most of the people I knew either made them or used them. Meth is the worst of them all. Once you get on it, you're hooked. You've got to have more and more, and you'll do anything to get it until only one thing matters in your life, and that's getting your next hit. This area is the meth capital of the world."

"I don't know what was in that backpack," Justin said. "But it had to be valuable. The bag was locked and sealed.

There was no way to open it without someone noticing. Richard threatened I'd end up at the bottom of the pond like the other two kids if I opened it or screwed with him. He said that others were involved, and they wouldn't stop with killing me. They would come after my family and friends."

"My God," Do you think Richard murdered those two kids?" Earl asked.

"I don't know. He might not even know anything about the murders, and he just wanted to scare me," Justin said.

"What kids in the pond? What are you talking about, Justin?" Dennis asked.

"Do you remember the storm we had late in summer, the time all the electricity went out on campus?"

"Yes, I remember," Dennis said.

"That night after the lights came on, I was lying in bed. I was in Rowlison Hall then. It was a really hot, muggy night. I had my dorm window open. It faced the pond. I was just about asleep when I heard a loud, grinding noise coming from the pond. It lasted only a minute or so. But not long after the noise stopped, I saw the red light shining through the window. I got up and looked out. The water spraying from the fountain was red, like blood. It only lasted for a few seconds, and then the lights of the fountain went out."

"I remember hearing stories of that from several students. No one believed the stories. Everyone assumed they were made up to scare the freshmen," Bobby said.

"Trust me. It happened," Justin said, grabbing for a fresh beer. "I went out the window that night. I needed to see what was going on. When I got close to the pond, I saw several men and three or four campus security guards. There were two row boats in the water. I saw them pull up what looked like two bodies wrapped in canvasses with ropes tied around them."

"Shit," Dennis said. "Why weren't there any news reports

about them? Why weren't the police called?"

"I don't know. But I suspect that the college tried to cover it up. The publicity would have been terrible for them," Justin said. "Besides, the boys that died in that pond weren't students."

"How do you know that?" Bobby asked.

"Because if they were students, the school wouldn't have been able to cover it up. Besides, I'm pretty sure that I know who they were. I saw posters of two boys that were missing from Branson. An article about them was in the Branson newspaper. The article speculated that they were involved in drugs. The article went on to say that the family had hired a private investigator that was looking into the disappearance."

"Drugs, I told you boys about how serious the problem is in the Ozarks," Bobby said. "I wouldn't be a bit surprised if those boys were murdered because of a drug deal that went wrong."

"Justin, I can only think of one reason someone would pay you $200 to deliver a package to St. Louis," Bobby said. "You were delivering drugs."

"I've thought about that, Bobby. You are probably right. But I don't know who I can trust. Mr. Gholson, the athletic director, hired me to drive busses. Richard said a lot of other people are involved. I'm afraid to approach him. He may be a part of it. I can't do anything until I know exactly what is going on and who is involved. Richard alluded to Tyler being involved. He has left school now. Then there was the other student bus driver that left school and died in a car accident. Whoever the people are that are involved are serious about protecting themselves."

"Well, one thing is for sure, buddy. You have four friends here that you can trust. We'll have your back," Earl said.

"Absolutely, Justin," Dennis said.

"I'm with you, too," Bobby said. "I know these hill people. They can be violent when protecting themselves. But most aren't the sharpest knives in the drawer. And almost all of them are a few fries shy of a happy meal, if you know what I mean. I think it's a result of generations of inner breeding," Bobby said.

CHAPTER 7
A LONG NIGHT

Justin, Earl, Bobby and Dennis finished the remainder of the beer. While they drank, they speculated about the murders and about the backpack. With each beer, they were building their courage.

"Let me ask you, buddy," Earl said. "Did you see a safe in the office or any place where evidence might be hidden?"

"I don't remember seeing a safe. The room was bare except for a desk and a table. I did see a door, though."

"I tell you, boys, we need to get inside that office," Bobby said.

It was just after 2am when one by one, the friends climbed out their dorm window and made their way down the fire escape. Outside it was a cold evening, temperatures dipping into the thirties. The moon was hidden behind a dense wall of clouds. A light fog had crept in from the lakes in the valley, limiting visibility to just a few feet. Even the lights of the fountain were skewed by the fog.

They walked quietly along the tree lines to the gravel road leading to the bus lot. Getting caught out after curfew would mean expulsion from S of O. No one wanted that. When they reached the gravel road, the boys walked the pastures alongside the road so as not to make noise.

The parking lot was dark and quiet. There were no lights

in the lot or the office. Six buses sat in the lot. It was Sunday morning. There would not be any early morning departures. S of O sports teams didn't schedule events on Sundays. It was God's Day.

"This is the best possible night to break into the office," Earl said. "The buses won't be going anywhere. The lot and the office should be quiet."

Earl was right. No one appeared to be around. But there was one thing no one in the group could be certain of. That was if there were security guards watching the lot.

"If there are drugs in that office, they would certainly take precautions, maybe alarms or security guards," Bobby said.

The group sat down in the tall grass next to the parking lot, listening and watching for any movement. The fog prohibited seeing the entire lot and the office, so no one could be certain the lot was completely abandoned. They moved into the lot using the buses to shield themselves from visibility in case someone was there.

Bobby took leadership of the group. It was a side of Bobby that the others had never seen before. He was a natural-born leader. Bobby had grown up in the hill country of the Ozarks. His family operated several stills on their property. They also grew weed. He had watched his father and two uncles take precautions so as not to be discovered. Three times police and federal agents had come in search of illegal stills and drugs. Stills had been discovered and destroyed. One of the marijuana fields had been burned down, but no one from the family had ever been caught. Bobby learned from his father and uncles how to hide, how to avoid the authorities, and how to protect others.

The group went from bus to bus, each time getting a little closer to the office. They stopped and waited each time, listening for any movement, watching for any people. The last bus was less than twenty feet from the office. They waited there the longest.

They had decent visibility of the office even through the fog. No lights were on inside the building. Shades were pulled on the two windows in the office.

Earl stayed back behind the bus to watch for anyone that might approach. He had his cell phone to call Bobby in case he needed to alert them to get out of the building.

Bobby found a window that wasn't securely locked. He was able to pry the lock open and lift the window to get inside. Justin and Dennis followed him through the window. Once inside, they shut the window and began looking around. Bobby had grabbed three flashlights before the group left Brown Hall. Ever since the electricity went off on campus earlier that summer, nearly all the students kept them in their rooms.

Inside the office, it was completely dark. The flashlights provided narrow beams of light. Bobby motioned for Dennis to check the desk. He motioned for Justin to check the cabinets behind the coffee machine. Bobby went to the door at the rear of the office. It was locked. He used a flathead screwdriver to try to pry the door away from the lock. But there was an additional deadbolt lock securing the door.

"Dennis, see if there is a key in that desk," Bobby said.

Dennis opened every drawer. There was no key. He did find a logbook, though. It listed dates, cities, and bus numbers. Several of the dates had been scratched off. There was a code at the end of each line. 1L50, 2.5L125, 20L,1000 so on.

"Hey, I found a logbook. What should I do with it?" Dennis asked.

"Take pictures of the pages with your cellphone," Bobby said.

"Hey, guys. The wall behind this cabinet sounds hollow when I hit it," Justin said.

"Hold on," Bobby said. "Let us help you with that."

Bobby, Dennis and Justin moved everything out of the

cabinet, including the shelves. Once the cabinet was empty, they pulled a false wall from the back of the cabinet, revealing a hollow space about 12" in diameter. Inside was a single key.

Justin reached in, grabbed the key and took it to the locked door. The key fit perfectly in the lock. He turned the key, and the door opened. Inside was a large steel safe. Bobby stepped inside. As soon as he did, an alarm went off. There was no time to replace the shelves and contents in the cabinet and put the key back. They barely had time to shut the door and climb out the window when Earl signaled the group that people were coming.

The group ran for hiding spots amongst the rows of buses just as two campus security cars pulled up in front of the office. Soon they were separated from each other. Each maintaining the same goal, get back to the dorm room without being spotted.

Two other campus security patrol cars pulled into the bus lot. One parked on the only road leading in and out of the lot, and the other parked at the rear of the parking lot. Both shined spotlights toward the buses.

The friends needed to find a way out quick before they were discovered. Each was on their own, splitting up when they ran from the office. Justin found himself hiding in the second row of buses. From where he was, he had a good view of the area in front of the office. Three trucks pulled up outside the office. Eight men with guns and flashlights got out of them. They formed a line from one end of the parking lot to the other and then began moving forward, flashlights pointed ahead, searching every part of the lot.

Those men aren't the campus police, Justin thought to himself. *Campus police don't carry guns. Besides, these men are dressed in work clothes, similar to what you would expect from a field hand at a farm to wear or possibly a hunter. They're wearing jeans, tee shirts and flannel shirts. Their boots are worker's boots, not cowboy boots. Two are wearing camouflage.*

They weren't students, and they weren't S of O employees.

Other than instructors, coaches and administrative personnel, S of O employed very few outsiders. Those that were employed had specialty jobs that students were unable to fill. All wore uniforms with S of O nametags which set them apart from the student workers. Besides, all S of O employees were well groomed with short hair that didn't touch the ears and no facial hair. They were required to follow the same dress code the students followed. These men looked rough, several with long hair, some with beards and facial hair. They weren't S of O employees.

About a quarter mile away, coming down the gravel road, were several more headlights. They were not the lights of cars or trucks, though. The headlights were closer together and lower to the ground. They were traveling two across down the gravel road.

Justin had to move. He had no choice. They would discover him soon. He moved away from the flashlights coming toward him. He could hear the buses in front of him being searched. He saw the beams from the flashlights going down each row of the two buses directly in front of him. He slowly and quietly moved toward the back of the parking lot. That's when he saw two campus security guards stationed at the back of the lot.

They are trying to surround the lot, Justin thought. *Soon, there will be no way to escape.*

Justin decided to escape to the Northeast section of the lot. It was the area that was farthest away from campus. That part of the lot backed up to cornfields. The fields had been harvested a month earlier but had not been plowed yet. The remaining stalks provided some cover, and with the light fog, Justin reasoned it was his best option to escape.

When he reached the Northeastern edge of the parking lot, he scanned the area for anyone. The area was completely dark.

He could see beams of light from flashlights in the distance but nothing close by. A barbed wire fence separated the parking lot from the cornfield. Justin removed his coat, draped it over the top of the fence and pushed down as far as he could.

That's when he heard it. "Stop," someone yelled.

Justin turned around and saw Earl running directly toward him. Then he saw flashlights about fifty feet away coming up directly behind Earl. Justin held the fence down as Earl ran toward it, hurdling the fence at the last minute.

"Come on, buddy. They are right behind me," Earl said to Justin.

Justin straddled the fence and pulled himself over to the other side. Quickly, he grabbed his coat and ran into the cornfield.

The two friends ran as fast as they could through the field. When they finally turned around, the flashlights were gone.

"Thank God for the coach's speed training," Earl said.

"Yeah, but my foot is killing me," Justin said.

"At least you're alive," Earl said. "Those guys looked pretty serious. Did you see the guns they were carrying?"

"Yeah, I saw them. I hope Bobby and Dennis got away."

"Well, we haven't heard gunfire. That's a good sign," Earl said.

"Do you have any idea where we are, Earl?"

"I think we are on the far eastern side of campus, past the farm and where the fields bump up to the woods leading down to the lake."

"How do we get back to the dorm from here?"

"We'd need to go back the way we came. I'm not sure that is a good option, given the fact that a dozen rednecks are searching for us in that direction."

"What if we continue on and head into the woods? We can circle around to the front of campus and get back that way?"

"Sounds like a plan to me," Earl said. "But it's going to

take us miles out of our way, and it will be daylight in another hour. We're going to need to run. Are you sure that your foot is up to it?"

"It's got to be. I don't see any other option. OK, let's go," Justin said.

Earl didn't answer. Instead, he put his index finger to his mouth, a gesture to signal Justin to be quiet. The two boys stood completely still.

There was a noise in the background. It sounded like an engine, several engines roaring from behind them. Then over a slight hill fifty yards behind them in the cornfield, several lights appeared. They weren't car lights. They were close together and low to the ground. The engines made a distinct noise.

"Those are ATVs," Earl said quietly. "Damn, they're looking for us."

The ATVs, six of them, were spread out across the cornfield, each with spotlights that were focused on the ground in front and to the sides of them. They were traveling at a slow speed.

"Let's get out of here," Justin said. Earl agreed. The men searching for them were about fifty yards away and closing in.

Justin and Earl ran toward the end of the cornfield. As they got closer, they saw a pasture between the cornfield and the fence. Beyond the fence was the woods. The cornfield had provided them some cover, but the pasture would not. The pasture was completely open, flat, and the grass was short. It had recently been cut.

When they reached the end of the cornfield, the men were at least a hundred yards behind them. They could see the searchlights in the distance.

"We've got to go for it, Justin," Earl said when they reached the pasture. "They'll be here in just a few minutes."

Justin agreed.

So, the boys ran a full-out sprint through the pasture. They reasoned that if they were spotted, they could beat the ATVs to the fence and into the woods. Midway through the open pasture, they were spotted by one of the men.

"They're running through the pasture," one of the men shouted to the others.

The ATVs took off full speed through the cornfield, with spotlights shining directly at the boys.

"They're gaining on us," Earl said, looking back.

When they got to the barbed wire fence, Earl took off his jacket and wrapped it around the top of the fence like Justin had done earlier. Then he pushed down on the wires as far as he could. But this time, a sharp wire penetrated his jacket and went into his hand.

"Damn," he yelled. That's my letterman jacket. The wire had ripped through his jacket and into the palm of his hand, causing blood to spill onto his jacket and on the fence.

Justin jumped the fence, followed by Earl. He grabbed his jacket and tried to pull it off the fence, but it was caught between several sharp wires. It wasn't coming off. The ATVs were getting close now. The spotlight was directly on him. He shielded his face from view with one hand while he pulled on the jacket with the other. It was no use. The jacket wasn't coming off the fence. So, he left it there, and the boys ran toward the woods. That's when they heard the gunfire. Justin heard a bullet whiz past his head and into a tree just past him. Earl ducked, making himself a smaller target as several shots hit around him.

They kept on running. The spotlights fixed directly on them as they ran into the woods. They kept running even after the lights from the searcher's ATVs disappeared. About ten minutes into the woods, they slowed to a fast walk. It was completely dark in the woods. The sun hadn't begun to come over the horizon, and the fog and clouds prevented the moon from providing any light.

They had no sense of direction, no idea where they were. The woods were dense. The only sounds other than their footsteps and heavy breathing were of birds and small critters that made the woods their home. It was frightening in the woods but safer than trying to go back.

"Damn, that was my letterman jacket that I left on the fence. Do you know how many extra hours I had to work to buy that?"

"No, but I'd be more concerned about your hand, Earl. That wound looks like it's going to need stitches," Justin said.

"Nah, I've had worse cuts than that. Clean it with some alcohol and bandage it, and it will be fine."

When Justin and Earl began descending through the woods, they reasoned that they were heading toward Lake Taneycomo. They knew the lake was located in the valley below the northeast section of campus. The fog that developed over the lake's surface often blanketed campus during the early morning hours of late summer and early fall. The western side of the lake was about three miles from campus. It was the uncommercialized side of the lake. Steep hills and rocky shores made that side useless for swimming or launching boats. But it was perfect for fishing and partying away from prying eyes. Its shores could be followed to several gravel and dirt roads. The roads were used by locals that visited the lake. The gravel roads could be used to get back to campus. Some students used the gravel roads to reach the lake and enjoy the privacy and seclusion that that side of the lake provided.

That section of the lake was best known for providing the seclusion that many young lovers sought. But it also was known for a private place to party. Most of those parties, it was rumored, had equal supplies of booze and drugs.

The fog was heaviest close to the banks of the lake. As the boys got closer, the fog was so thick it dropped visibility to within a few feet. Justin was the first to notice the light off to the south. It illuminated the fog just above the tree line.

"What do you think that is?" Justin asked.

"I don't know," Earl said. "But I think we need to stay clear of it. We need to get back to campus."

A few yards ahead of them was a path going in the direction of the light. Justin took the path over Earl's objections.

"We can make better time by going on the path," Justin insisted.

The boys took that path. A hundred yards down the path, they could make out the outlines of a building surrounded by trees. The building, maybe thirty feet long, built of wood, looked a lot like a warehouse. Lights were on inside, but the windows were shaded. Outside was a three-sided wood shed that appeared to contain four large generators. The noise from the generators had somehow been muffled. They could be heard but only from a short distance away. Three smokestacks were protruding from the roof, emitting a dark, gray smoke that mixed with the fog and created a yellowish glow just above the tree lines.

"That must be what we saw," Justin said. "It's an odd place to put a building."

"Not if you're trying to hide from the outside world," Earl said. "I'm telling you, Justin, this is someone's property, and hill people aren't too kind to trespassers. I think we need to get out of here."

"What do you think someone's doing this far in the woods, away from any roads?" Justin asked.

"Damn, you're naïve, buddy," Earl said. "I've seen a few of these places before, not as large as this, but just as secluded. Hill people and drug dealers build them to make meth. We've stumbled on to a meth lab. We need to get the hell out of here. If they spot us, they won't think twice about killing us."

They turned to walk away. That's when Justin felt the wire.

His left foot caught the bottom of it just as he turned around. An alarm sounded. Large, bright lights came on from the area around the building.

"Shit, we've got to get out of here quick," Earl said.

Justin started running down the path.

"Stop, Justin. They'll be looking for us on the path. We've got to go through the woods. No paths or roads," Earl said.

"Then, how do we get out of here?" Justin asked.

"Through the woods, buddy, toward the lake. How good of a swimmer are you, Justin?"

"Oh shit, not very good."

"Well, it looks like now is a good time to learn," Earl said.

The sun was just beginning to come up over the horizon. Soon it would be daylight and more difficult to hide. In all the excitement, the boys had lost their sense of direction. The sunrise was a blessing for them. They used the sun to guide them to the southeast, to the lake. The terrain was steep the closer they got. Running was impossible. They had to slow their pace to navigate the steep decline and the large rocks that littered the landscape.

In the background, Justin could hear dogs approaching from behind, through the woods, through the same path they had taken.

"The dogs have our scent," Earl said. "From the sounds of their barks, it won't take them very long to catch us."

They hurried as best they could. Soon the lake was in their sight, not more than sixty yards away. Soon the tree line gave way to large rocks that covered the last few yards of ground just before the edge of the water. The dogs were much closer now. Men could be heard following them.

The rocks were damp and slippery. Justin maneuvered over the first several without trouble. Then, his left foot slipped. It slid off one rock and fell in between two others. It happened to be the place where a large rattlesnake was nestled. He felt the bite.

It felt like a small knife cutting through his ankle. He jumped, losing his balance and hitting several rocks before tumbling into the water. Earl dove in after him. He grabbed Justin underneath his arms and lifted him to the water's surface.

"Are you OK, buddy?"

"No, I've been bitten by a rattlesnake."

That's when they saw the first dog come out of the trees and onto the rocks above them.

"We've got to get out of here. Can you swim?" Earl asked.

"I can try."

"Hold onto my shoulder. I'll help you," Earl said.

They began to swim slowly across the lake. Soon the dogs were at the edge of the water. By the time the men that were following them reached the edge of the lake, Justin and Earl were out of sight.

Twenty minutes into the swim, Justin's ankle had swollen to twice its normal size. The poison was moving through his body.

"It hurts, Earl. I'm not sure that I can make it," Justin said.

"Yes, you can. You made it up and down Outlook Mountain in that weighted backpack, didn't you? A little snake bite isn't going to stop you," Earl said.

Earl's words were optimistic, but his mind knew better. Ozark rattlesnakes were some of the deadliest snakes. Left untreated, most people would not survive more than an hour. It had already been nearly thirty-minutes, and they were less than halfway across the lake.

***

Earl spotted the fishing boat. It was coming out from a dock on the other side of the lake. He shouted and waved his hands. What seemed like several minutes went by with no acknowledgement from the person in the boat, and finally, he saw his hand lift up and wave. The boat turned toward the boys.

A couple of minutes later, the boat pulled up alongside them.

Earl lifted Justin up to the boat. The fisherman inside it pulled him onboard. Then Earl climbed into the small bass boat. Justin was unconscious. His head was on fire, and his ankle was swollen to at least three times its normal size. A large blue puffy patch was slowly moving its way up his leg.

"Do you have a knife?" Earl asked the man.

He nodded his head.

"Then give it to me," Earl said.

Earl took the knife and cut a deep mark in Justin's ankle right in the area of the bite marks. He moved the knife downward and cut another line upward, creating an "X" cut. Then he lowered his mouth to the opening he had created and sucked about a dozen times. After each suck, he spit the blood and poison out of his mouth into the lake. When he was finished, he took two rags the fisherman had in his boat and tied one tightly just below the bite marks and one just above. Earl looked at his friend. Justin was still unconscious.

"Do you have a cellphone?" Earl asked the man.

"Yes, I do," he replied.

"Then call 911. Tell them my friend was bitten by a rattlesnake. Have an ambulance meet us at the dock and tell them to bring anti-venom for the snake bite."

A few minutes after the boat docked, the ambulance arrived. Two paramedics jumped out, and one administered the anti-venom. They lifted Justin onto a cot and rolled him into the ambulance. Earl rode with him to the hospital.

"Hang on, buddy," he said. "You're going to be fine in a day or two."

"But Justin didn't respond. He didn't move. His color had turned a light shade of blue. He looked like he was close to death. The paramedic hooked oxygen up to him and ran an IV medicine into his veins.

Earl, not much of a believer in the power of prayer, prayed nonetheless.

CHAPTER 8
HEALING THE WOUNDS

Justin was in the hospital for nearly three weeks. He spent the first week in intensive care. Doctors said he was on the edge of death. They said that he nearly lost his leg. He was in an induced coma for the first three days. When he woke up on the fourth day, his parents were by his bedside.

"Honey, we were so worried about you," his mother said, putting her arms around him and hugging him. "What happened? The doctors only told us that you were bit by a rattlesnake."

"We drove down the first day you were here," his father said. "Karl Gholson with the school called and told us about the accident. Your mother and I were worried sick about you. All Mr. Gholson said was that you were bitten by a rattlesnake and were in the Branson Hospital. When we got here, the doctors told us how serious it was. You're one lucky guy, Justin. They got you to the hospital just in time."

"Have you spoken to Earl?" Justin asked his parents.

"No, who's Earl?"

"Never mind. He's one of my friends. I thought he might have stopped in to see me."

"No, nobody's been here except a cute young girl. I think she said her name was Risa. She came by yesterday, but you were still in a coma. She said that she would come back. She seemed very worried about you," his mother said. "Are you dating her?"

"Not really. Why did she say something?"

"No, I was just curious. She seemed very nice," his mother said with a smile.

"Dad, did Mr. Gholson say anything to you about what happened to me?"

"No, he wasn't sure himself. He said that you had left campus sometime Saturday night. He had heard that you were going fishing. He assumed that you were bit by the snake at the lake and managed to flag down a fisherman in his boat to get you to the hospital. He really didn't know anything else."

"Dad, did he say if I was with anybody?"

"No. He seemed to think you were by yourself. Were you with someone else, son?"

"No, I don't think so. My memory is a little foggy."

"We'll let you rest a little bit. Your mom and I are going to be here for several more days. Mr. Gholson booked us a room at the hotel down the road from campus. The school is paying for the room and all our expenses. Mr. Gholson said not for you to worry about classes. He notified all your instructors, and you can start back to class whenever you are ready."

"Justin, we love you, and we'll be back to see you in the morning," his mother said as she gave him one more hug.

When they were gone, Justin sat in the hospital bed thinking about what his parents had said. There was no mention of Earl being with him. *Why was that?* he thought. Karl Gholson told his parents that he had gone fishing. *Does he know what happened that night?*

Most of all, Justin was worried for his friends, Earl, Dennis and Bobby. Did they get back to campus, OK? *Why hadn't Karl Gholson mentioned them?* he wondered. Then he noticed two vases of flowers on his nightstand. They both had cards. He picked up the first card. It was from S of O.

"Best wishes for a speedy recovery." Signed Coach Moffitt

and every member of the cross-country team, including Bobby, Dennis and Earl.

The card attached to the second vase of flowers said, "My heart nearly broke when I heard what happened to you," Love, Risa.

Justin couldn't help but smile. He cared deeply for Risa, and he knew that she felt the same way about him.

A few minutes later, a nurse came in with a pill to help him rest. Shortly after that, Justin was asleep. But it wasn't a restful sleep. His mind wandered to the events that led him to the hospital. He thought of his friends. He thought of the escape from the bus lot. He thought about the office and what they had discovered. He thought about the predicament he was in. He wondered how much danger he was in.

Justin tossed and turned that night. His nightmares were vivid. The pill he was given made it difficult to wake from the nightmares. Although he tried several times during the night. Finally, the sunlight pouring through the hospital room window began to shake him from his stupor. As he began to wake, a warm feeling came across him. He felt more relaxed, more comfortable. He felt a warm hand touching his, tightening slightly as he began to wake. He felt another hand touching his cheek softly, slowly rubbing it up and down. He felt a tender kiss on his lips.

When his eyes opened, a sheriff was sitting next to him. "How are you doing, son?" the sheriff said.

"Fine, I guess. Why are you here, sheriff?"

"Well, son, my name is Sheriff Roscoe Dale. I'm the sheriff of Branson. You caused quite a stir around here, son. Can you tell me what happened to you?"

"I got bit by a rattlesnake," Justin said.

"Yeah, I gathered that, boy. What I'm curious about is what you were doing on the banks of that lake in the middle of the night?"

"I was fishing, sheriff."

"Yeah, that's what I heard, but it seems kind of odd that a college boy would break curfew to wander down to the lake by himself late at night. Are you sure that you went there to fish?"

"Yes, sheriff. That's why I went to the lake."

"Strange, though," the sheriff said, rubbing his chin. "We searched the banks of that lake and didn't find a fishing rod or any tackle."

"Well, it must have fallen in the lake with me after I got bit by the snake. I really don't remember, sheriff."

"Yeah, that's what I figured. You know it's funny," the sheriff said with a smile. "There was a disturbance in a parking lot on the campus of S of O the same night of your accident. Two boys were caught. They said they were alone. They happened to be roommates of yours. I believe their names are Dennis and Bobby. They are in a world of trouble with the school. I wouldn't be a bit surprised if they get expelled, breaking curfew and all. You seemed to break curfew that night, too. You don't happen to know anything about the disturbance that night, do you?"

"No, sheriff. I don't know anything about it."

"Well, son, if you happen to hear something or remember something you might have seen that night, you'll be sure and tell me, won't you?"

"Yes, sheriff."

"Good."

The sheriff got up and walked out without saying another word.

Justin was shaking beneath the covers of his bed.

Sheriff Dale was an intimidating person, standing well over six feet tall, heavy built with a look of a man that didn't take crap from anyone.

A few minutes after the sheriff left, Risa walked into the room. She smiled tenderly when she saw him. Then she rubbed a tear from her cheek, and her smile turned to a frown.

"Damn you, Justin. Damn you," she said. "You scared the shit out of me. Don't ever do that again."

Justin smiled. "I won't," he said. "How'd you know that I was here?"

"Well, silly. It's a small town and an even smaller campus. Word gets around fast."

"No, really, who told you, Risa?"

"Earl told me. I left a note for you to meet me by the fountain two days ago. He read it. Imagine my surprise when he was waiting on the bench by the fountain. He told me you went fishing at the lake and were bitten by a rattlesnake. I knew you didn't fish. I told him that his story was bullshit. But he stuck with it. Tell me, Justin, what really happened?"

"Risa, trust me when I tell you that I can't say," he said.

"Damn it, Justin. I love you. You need to be able to tell me anything. No matter what happened, I'll understand. Was it another girl? I know what goes on at that side of the lake. It's either partying or sex. I never thought of you as a party person, so was it a girl?"

"No, it wasn't a girl."

"Good, because I'm afraid I'd have to beat her up."

"You know, I don't really see you as a fighter, Risa."

"Well, just don't get involved with another girl, and you won't ever know." She smiled, lowered her face to Justin's and gave him a long, tender kiss. "I love you, Justin."

"I love you too, Risa."

"What's going on with Richard?" Justin asked.

"Talk about spoiling the moment. Why did you need to bring him up?"

"Because I care about you, that's why."

"Well, he and I aren't seeing each other right now."

"Why?"

"We had a fight. He was so controlling. He kept me at that condo and wouldn't let me leave except to go to classes, and even then, he or one of his friends had to take me and bring me back afterward. I was like a prisoner."

"Yeah, but it had been that way for a while, Risa. What made you get away from him?"

"He hit me, Justin. We had a huge fight. He was mad, more upset than I had ever seen him. He slapped me and pushed me against the wall. That was the last straw. I walked out and came back to campus."

"When did that happen?"

"Two days ago. Right after I heard that you were in the hospital. I told him that I wanted to see you. I told him how much I cared about you. He got really upset."

"So, are you done with him, Risa?"

"Yes, I can never go back to someone that is that jealous and that controlling."

"I'm happy to hear that, Risa."

"I thought you would be," Risa said with a smile. "Now you just need to get well and get out of this hospital so we can spend some quality time together."

Risa visited Justin the next two evenings after classes. Justin's parents were there, too. They got to know Risa. She was charming to them, but there was something that bothered his mother about her, something that she just couldn't put her finger on.

Justin sensed his mother's uneasiness when Risa was around.

"What's wrong, Mom?" Justin asked.

"I don't know exactly," she said. "There's just something about her. She's almost too nice. It's like she is trying too hard."

"She's probably just a little nervous around you, mom. She's just trying to make a good impression," Justin said.

"You're probably right, honey. Still, did you notice the high school ring she is wearing on her right hand?"

"Yeah, so what? It's her high school ring."

"No, it's a man's high school ring," his mother said.

"I guess that I never thought about it. She's worn that ring ever since I met her. I think it is her ex-boyfriend's ring."

"Well, honey. Don't you find it odd that she says that she broke up with her boyfriend, but she still wears his ring?"

Justin's father gave his wife a stern look. "Honey, I'm sure there is a perfectly good reason for it. I recall you wearing a necklace that was given to you by your ex long after you started dating me."

Justin's mother began to smile. "Yes, you're probably right," she said.

"What was his name, anyway? Clive or Homer?"

"It was Steve. You know that."

"Yeah, that's right. By the way, whatever happened to that necklace?"

"I sold it in a garage sale a long time ago."

"Good," his father said with a smile.

The evening before Justin was to be released from the hospital, Coach Moffit came to visit him along with the entire team. It was good to see everyone, including Earl, Bobby and Dennis. He had so many questions for his friends. But that night was not the time to ask those questions. The team brought pizza. They ate, laughed and talked about classes and the upcoming District competition. They did not talk about the night at the bus lot. No one asked about what led up to the snake bite. No one asked why he chose to swim across the lake to get help rather than go back to campus.

Risa did not stop by his hospital room that night. Justin assumed that Earl or one of his other teammates told her the team was going to visit Justin, and that's why she chose not to visit him that night.

But, when she didn't show up the next morning when he was scheduled to be released, he became concerned.

His parents were there to drive him back to campus. It was a Saturday. The campus was quiet. His teammates were away at the district competition. Justin got settled into his room. He gave his parents a tour of the campus. Then they went to dinner. Still, there was no sign of Risa. She wasn't there to welcome him back. There wasn't a note waiting for him when he returned to his room.

At dinner, his mom asked about Risa.

"I was surprised Risa wasn't at the hospital when you were checked out this morning," his mother said.

"I'm sure that she wanted to. She probably couldn't get off work," Justin said, trying to come up with a viable explanation.

"How serious are you both?" his mother asked.

"I don't know, Mom. We care a lot about each other. Why do you ask?"

His mother smiled. But it was more of a forced smile than a natural one. "I'm just curious. She seems nice. I was just wondering if you're in love with her."

The look on his mother's face gave him the first feeling that she wasn't comfortable with Risa. He decided not to tell his mother the truth. "No, I don't think so. We're just good friends. I care for her, and she cares for me. But I don't think we're in love, not yet anyway."

That night after dinner, his parents dropped him off at the front gate of the campus. They would have driven him to Brown Hall, but he wanted to walk. They hugged and said their goodbyes, and Justin's parents drove back home. Thanksgiving was only three weeks away, and Justin promised to come home for the long weekend.

It was an unusually warm night for early November, cool

but not cold, with a light breeze. There wasn't a cloud in the sky. The stars were bright, and the moon was large. He took his time walking back, enjoying the scenery. S of O was beautiful at night. The leaves on the trees were turning. The lighted white stoned buildings, the glow from the fountain at the center of the campus, and the brick walkways dotted with turn-of-the-century light posts were reminiscent of a Norman Rockwell painting. *Damn, it feels good to be alive*, he thought.

His leg had completely healed. It felt good. The walk felt good. A light breeze sent a slight chill through his body. At that moment in time, Justin felt invincible. He felt full of life. He had cheated death. That had empowered him. It had given him the desire to make the most of life, to chase his dreams. He wanted to tell Risa how he felt. He wanted her to know how much he cared for her.

Students had gathered around the pond and outside both dormitories that night to enjoy the unusually warm evening. It felt more like early September than early November. A few spotted him. They told him they were glad he was back. Several asked what had happened to him.

He just smiled and said, "I wasn't watching where I was going and stepped on a snake."

He didn't want anyone to know the whole story. The men who chased him probably already suspected he was one of the boys they were chasing. Word of what had happened to him was all over the small campus.

Justin was nearly back to Brown Hall when his mind wandered to Risa. He wondered why she hadn't come to see him that day. She knew that he was being discharged. She had promised to be there when he left. He looked over at Claire Hall. He wondered if she was there. Justin decided to find out. He walked to her dormitory. There were about three dozen students outside, enjoying the nice evening. He scanned the crowd looking for Risa. She wasn't there. So, he went inside, up to the reception desk.

A young, thin girl with long, dark hair was behind the counter.

"Hello, Justin. I'm glad to see that you're OK," she said.

He didn't recognize her. "Thank you," he said. "I'm sorry. What's your name?" he asked with a smile.

"I'm Katy," she said. "I'm in your Chemistry class. I sit a few rows behind you."

"Gosh, I'm sorry. I didn't recognize you."

"That's OK. We've never actually talked before," she said with a smile. "How can I help you?"

"I'd like to see Risa Johnson if she's in."

The look on Katy's face changed. "I'm sorry, Justin. I guess you didn't know. Risa dropped out of school today. She's gone."

"Are you sure?"

"Yes, I'm positive. My room is on the same floor as hers. I saw her boyfriend, Richard and several of her friends moving her stuff out of her room early this morning. I asked Richard what was going on, and he told me that Risa had dropped out of school and was moving back to Sikeston."

"Katy, did Risa leave me a note?"

"She didn't leave one here," she said. "Maybe she left one for you at your dorm."

"No, I've been there. She didn't leave me anything."

"It's probably none of my business, Justin, but Risa seems pretty committed to Richard. She talked about him all the time. She even wears his ring. You seem like a nice guy, Justin. Maybe, it's best for you that she is gone."

Justin forced a smile, turned and walked out of Claire Hall. He couldn't help but wonder if it was Risa's decision to leave. He didn't think so. *She couldn't possibly have faked the feelings she showed toward me*, Justin thought. He knew she was in love with him. He knew that she wouldn't leave without talking to him. He knew she would have at least left him a note. Justin was convinced that she was forced to leave campus. He was equally convinced that he was the reason she left.

There was a question he needed to ask Katy. Justin turned around and walked back into Claire Hall and up to the reception desk.

"Well, it's good to see you again, Justin, although I didn't think I would see you so soon," Katy said.

"I forgot to ask you something, Katy."

"What is it, Justin?"

"When you saw Richard and his friends moving stuff out of Risa's room, did you see Risa?"

"No, I didn't see her. Maybe she was outside."

"When was the last time you saw her?"

"Last week, in World History class. She sits a couple of seats across from me."

"Did you talk to her?"

"No. She was late arriving in class and left right afterward. Come to think of it, I remember Richard was waiting for her outside of the classroom. They left together."

"When was the last time you saw her in the dormitory?"

"Hey, what is this, Justin. You sound like a detective investigating a crime?"

"No, I'm just trying to figure out what is going on."

"Well, I can assure you there is nothing unusual going on. She's in love with Richard and probably left school to be with him. I've heard he spends a lot of time at a condo in Branson. I think she either went back to Sikeston to be with her family, or she moved into that condo."

"You're probably right, but still, I'd like to talk to her roommate."

"Risa doesn't have a roommate. Since the beginning of

the semester, she has had a room to herself. Most of the girls are jealous of her, including me. She's the only girl in Claire Hall that has a room to herself. Some of the freshmen even sleep three to a room."

"I don't suppose you could take me to her room and let me look inside?" Justin asked.

Katy laughed. "You know the rules, Justin. No boys are allowed upstairs. You'd get us both kicked out of school. Besides, you won't find anything. Everything is gone except the bed and desk. I looked inside after Richard and his friends left."

"Would you do me a favor, Katy?" Justin asked.

"Depends on the favor," Katy replied.

"When you can, could you go into her room and look around? See if she left anything behind?"

"Why would I do that?" she asked, "I barely know you."

"Because I can tell that you're a good, caring person, and if something bad did happen to Risa, you would want to help her."

"OK, I'll do it but only because of that silly puppy-dog look on your face. I'm telling you that you should just forget about Risa. You deserve a girl that is caring and knows what a good person you are, Justin."

"That sounds good. Do you know a girl like that?"

"Maybe," she said with a smile.

CHAPTER 9
THE DISAPPEARANCE OF RISA

Justin returned to Brown Hall a little past 10pm. His teammates had returned thirty minutes earlier from the district meet. Everyone was waiting in the common room of their suite when Justin returned.

The mood was somber. Although everyone welcomed him back, Justin could tell something bad had happened.

"Come on guys, what's up?" Justin asked.

Earl was the one that spoke up. "Buddy, I hate to tell you, but you've been kicked out of Brown Hall. You're supposed to report tomorrow to the housing director. They're going to put you back in Rowlison Hall."

"Why?" Justin asked with a shocked look on his face.

"Karl Gholson told Coach Moffitt that because of your injury, you weren't able to participate with the team, so you should not be in the athletic dorm. Coach was very upset. He argued for you. But Karl Gholson is the athletic director. His decision is the way it has to go."

"That just doesn't make sense, Earl. My foot is healing. I'll be completely healthy for track practice next semester."

"That's not the only thing, Justin," Earl said. "You're no longer going to drive the team to our meets. We're being assigned a new bus driver."

"Damn, so I won't be able to see you guys compete for the

rest of the season."

"Tell him the rest," Bobby said to Earl.

"What else?" Justin asked.

"Coach was told that he could not allow you to run track or cross-country for S of O. He was also told that none of the members of our team are to have any contact with you. We're not supposed to spend time with you. We can't even talk to you," Earl said.

"That doesn't make sense," Justin said. "Why would they do this to me?"

"It's not them, Justin. It is Karl Gholson. You need to talk to him. He wants to see you first thing in the morning," Earl replied.

That's when Earl handed him a handwritten note. As he did, Earl put his index finger over his lips to indicate that he shouldn't say a word. The note said:

The room is bugged. We are being listened to. Don't say anything else. I'll get a hold of you when it is safe to talk.

After showing Justin the note, Earl took it away. He went into the kitchen, turned the stove on and burned the note.

The next morning Justin woke and went straight to the athletic building. Coach Moffit was waiting for him outside the building.

"I'm sorry, Justin. I'm afraid that you have been cut from the cross-country and track teams. I want you to know that it wasn't my decision, but there is nothing that I can do about it. I wish you the very best, son. You're a good kid. Maybe, you'd be better off leaving S of O after this semester. A good friend of mine is the head coach of the track and cross-country teams at Missouri Western. He needs another good runner. He told me he has a scholarship waiting for you if you want it. They've got a young but very good program. I think it would be a good fit for you, Justin."

"Thanks, coach," Justin said with a tear in his eye.

Coach Moffit handed Justin a slip of paper with the Missouri Western coach's contact information. They shook hands, and Coach Moffit walked away.

Justin put the piece of paper in his pants pocket and walked inside the athletic building. Karl Gholson was waiting for him in his office.

"Justin, come on in. We need to talk," he said. Justin walked into the office and took a seat. "Welcome back, son," he said with a smile. "We were all worried about you. Rattlesnakes in the Ozarks can be deadly. You're very lucky."

"Yes, sir," Justin said.

"Well, I'll cut to the chase, Justin. You're being cut from the cross-country and track teams. In fact, I wouldn't try out for any sports at S of O. I've got a feeling you wouldn't make any of our teams."

"Why are you doing this, Mr. Gholson?" Justin asked.

"Well, let's just say that we've got very high standards for our athletes at S of O, and you just didn't reach them."

"I'm a strong runner, Mr. Gholson. I've done everything Coach Moffit has asked of me. I deserve to be on the team."

Karl Gholson's look changed. His face tightened. It turned red with anger. "Damn it, Justin. This has nothing to do with your running ability. You've broken our rules. We know what you were up to the night you got bit by the snake. Do you think we're stupid? You were at the bus lot that night. You broke into the building. We know you went through the drawers. We know that you saw things that you shouldn't have. You're in deep shit, boy."

"I don't know what you are talking about, Mr. Gholson," Justin said.

Karl Gholson smiled. "OK, I guess if I was in the same situation you're in, I would deny being there too." Then Karl

Gholson's tone softened. "You know, Justin, life can be a lot more pleasant for you at S of O if you'd just play ball. Hell, you might even be able to stay in Brown Hall. You might even be able to run track next semester. You'd find that if you befriend the right people on campus, life can be quite enjoyable here."

"And what do I need to do to make that happen," Justin asked.

"You need to tell me what you were looking for in that transportation building, you need to tell me exactly what you saw, and you need to give me everything you took from that building."

"As I told you before, Mr. Gholson, I didn't break into that building, and I have no idea who did."

"Well, that's too bad, Justin. I think we're done here for now. You need to report to the housing director. I believe he has a new room assignment for you. Also, report to the employment office. I believe they have a new job assignment for you. Have you ever cleaned up in a slaughterhouse before? I understand it is not a very desirable job." Then he waved his hand for Justin to leave.

That day he moved back to Rowlison Hall. He was assigned a room on the fifth floor, next to the freight elevator. He shared the room with a sophomore named Clay Robbins. Clay was a good old boy from Poplar Bluff, Mo. His previous roommate had quit school a week earlier.

Clay was a happy-go-lucky person. He didn't seem to take anything very seriously, including his classwork. His grades didn't seem to worry him, though. Clay was more interested in having a good time. The room was a mess. Clothes were laying everywhere, and food wrappers were on the beds. There were even several empty beer cans lying around.

"You know that if someone reports you for those beer cans, you get thrown out of school," Justin told him.

"Nobody will," Clay replied. "I don't bother anybody, and they don't bother me. You should know how things work around here by now. Mind your own business, and don't embarrass the school, and they'll leave you alone," he said.

Clay was quite a character. He looked a lot like a young Jim Nabors, and he talked a lot like him too. His smile was contagious. He was a simple, good-hearted person that you couldn't help but like. He wore a crew cut, a hairstyle that went out of style fifty years earlier. He adhered to the campus dress code when he went to classes and to church, but otherwise, he wore blue jean overalls with a white tee shirt and boots. He talked with a slow southern drawl that made him sound a bit dimwitted. But Justin learned quickly that Clay was very intelligent. Everything with him was an act. He acted the way he wanted people to perceive him. He found life to be more enjoyable when others didn't expect much from him.

Justin and Clay came from two totally different backgrounds. They were nearly exact opposites. Yet, in a short time, they became best friends. Both were outcasts. Few students dared to talk to Justin. Few students had any interest in talking to Clay. They were trouble. They were going in a direction that no one else wanted to go. They were roommates for a purpose. Both were not expected to stay at S of O beyond that semester.

It was Clay that found the bug in their room. It was a sensitive listening device that was planted inside the lampshade on their desk. Clay didn't remove it. Instead, he told Justin about it on their walk to work the day after discovering the device.

"We are being listened to, buddy," he said. "I found a bug in our lamp. There may be more. I don't know. What have you done, Justin? I know they aren't listening to me. So, it must be something you've done."

That's when Justin told him about the night in the bus lot. Clay didn't seem surprised.

"Describe the place you found in the woods," Clay said to Justin. "It's meth," he said. "They're operating a meth lab off campus. I'm sure of it," he said. "Meth's big in the Ozarks. When my granddad was young, he ran moonshine. That was the big thing during prohibition and for years afterward. Then it was marijuana. The Ozark dirt is prime for growing weed. Now it's meth. We have some of the best cooks around. I guess it's from our days of cooking moonshine. And the Ozarks are a great hiding place for the labs.

"Someone in the transportation department must be involved. That's why they came after you, buddy. Hell, you're lucky that you got away. But I don't think you're out of trouble. They must suspect you. Otherwise, they wouldn't have kicked you off the team, sent you to room with me and given you the shittiest job on campus."

"There's more," Justin said to Clay. "I know how they are moving the meth to their buyers. They're using the buses that take the sports teams to their events."

"How do you know that?" Clay asked.

"I was one of the bus drivers. I only made one delivery, and I didn't know what I was carrying on the bus, but I am convinced that is the way they move the meth from campus to their sellers."

"Then you must know who is involved?" Clay asked.

"I know two of them. One is Risa's boyfriend, Richard. He was the one that gave me instructions for delivering the package and he was the one that paid me a $200 bonus for delivering it. The other person is Karl Gholson, the athletic director. He was the one that gave me the bus driving job, and he was the one that threatened me when I got out of the hospital. He wanted to know what I saw and what I took from the building."

"What did you take?"

"Nothing, as far as I know. One of the guys took some pictures but as far as I know, that was all."

"Well, they must think that you took something important,"
Clay said. "Otherwise, I think you'd be dead, buddy, like those
two boys they found in the pond on campus."

Justin stopped walking. He had a shocked look on his
face. "How do you know about those boys? I didn't think anyone
knew about those bodies."

"I knew both those boys. They worked at the meth lab that
you discovered in the woods. Hell, I used to party with them last
summer. They were good old boys, grew up in the hills, a couple
of fries short of a happy meal, but good guys. I met them at a
party down by the lake. Damn, they liked to party. They could
drink more than anyone that I ever knew. Trouble was when
they were shit-faced, they talked too much. I assumed that was
what got them murdered. They told me about the meth lab. They
even took me there one night. We didn't get close enough to be
spotted, but we got close enough for me to tell that they weren't
full of shit.

"I was partying with them the night they disappeared.
They were shit-faced as usual when they started talking about
the meth lab again. But this time, I suspect, they were talking to
the wrong people. Two guys asked the boys to show them the
lab. That was the last time anyone saw them."

"How'd you know they were in the pond?" Justin asked.

"I partied too late that night. The campus was locked down.
I figured that I'd spend the night by the lake. I'd done it several
times before. But that night, there was a hell of a storm. I was
getting soaked outside in the woods. The thunder and lightning
were terrible that night. One bolt of lightning stuck close by.
I decided to sneak back on campus. By the time I got close to
campus, the rain had stopped. That's when the fog moved in. It
was thick that night. I figured that I may as well continue back to
campus. The chances of being spotted in that fog were slim, and
besides, I needed a decent night's sleep. I had a work assignment

later that morning. So, I continued toward the campus. All the lights were out. I assumed the lightning must have knocked out the electricity on campus. I was close to the pond when the lights came back on. I heard an awful noise come from the fountain. Soon after, I saw the fountain water turn pink and then red. I started toward the fountain when I saw two campus security police cars arrive. I hid behind a tree line and watched. I saw more men come to the pond. I saw them launch two or three row boats into the water. I saw them pull up the two canvases. I knew immediately who those bodies were. Those two boys had told me once that they had been threatened with being drowned in that pond if they ever told anyone about the lab."

"Who threatened them, Clay?"

"They didn't say. Buddy, if I were you, I'd get a long way away from S of O. They're not going to leave you alone until they get what they want."

"Clay, why do you think they decided to room us together?"

"I'm not sure," Clay said. "It could be completely by chance. My roommate had left school. I had an empty bed. Or, it could be," Clay said with a smile, "that I'm working for Karl Gholson, and they roomed you with me so I could find out what you had taken."

"That's not funny, Clay."

"No, but it is a possibility. You really don't know who to trust, buddy."

"I'll tell you why I think they put us together, Clay. I think they suspect you of knowing about their operation, too. Have you noticed all the security cameras around campus, Clay? Not to mention the security cameras around the meth lab. Maybe they know that you know about the drugs. Maybe they know both of us were at the pond that night the boys were pulled from it. Maybe they put us together on purpose, hoping we would talk in our room and share what we knew. How long do you think that bug had been there?"

"I have no idea, Justin."

"Don't you find it strange that you can drink in your room, leave beer cans sitting around and not get caught? Hell, anyone else would have been thrown out of school. The floor monitors do regular, unannounced inspections of all the rooms. They would have surely reported you for the beer. That's a clear violation of school rules. There is no way the administration would let that slide. I think they are using you to find out what both of us know."

"Hell," Justin said. "I think we're both in the same boat, and that boat has a slow leak."

"Not necessarily, buddy. We've got one big advantage. We know our room is bugged. Who is to say that we can't use that listening device to our advantage?"

"What do you have in mind, Clay?"

"I'm not sure yet, but I think it's a good idea to act like we never saw that bug, at least until we can find a way to use it to help us."

"Clay, I don't think they are just listening to us. I think they are watching us too. I don't know that for sure, but I have a feeling we are being watched."

"Me too, buddy."

For days, the two roommates continued their normal routine. They ate meals together in the cafeteria. They went to class and went to work together. They were outcasts. Few students talked to them even Justin's former teammates ignored him. Both had been assigned work in the slaughterhouse. They walked to work together and walked back together. If they needed to talk about something they couldn't discuss in their room, they would do it during their walks to or from the slaughterhouse. Both were convinced that they were being followed. There was something else too. Someone had been in their room. Stuff had been moved.

They were looking for something, or maybe they were just hoping to find something.

"I think it's time we took advantage of the bug in our room. We need to feed them something," Clay said on the walk back from the slaughterhouse. "We need to give them something that will show us they believe what we say and that we aren't aware of the listening device."

"Yeah, but what do we give them? What they really care about is who was with me when we broke into the transportation office, and I sure as hell can't give them that," Justin said.

"They also want to know what you saw when you were in that office," Clay said. "Isn't there something you can give them?"

Justin thought for a minute. Then he remembered. "The key to the hidden room in the office, I took it. We were in a hurry to get out of the office when the alarm went off, and I stuck the key into my pants pocket. It might still be in them. I brought the pants back from the hospital. They're in my dorm room, in the closet. I haven't checked them since I got back from the hospital."

"Shit, buddy. If the key is still there, that's what we can use to see if they're still listening to us."

"I'll check inside the pants pocket when we get back," Justin said.

"Yes, and if it's there, you can tell me you found it inside the room. Then, say that you are going to put it in the desk drawer. Put it there, and if it's gone tomorrow, we'll know they are still listening to us," Clay said.

When they got back to their dormitory room, Justin went directly to the closet. He found the pants he was wearing that night. He put his hand inside the right front pocket and pulled out the key. He lifted it and showed it to Clay then he spoke.

"Damn, look what I found, Clay," Justin said loud enough for the listening device to pick it up.

"It's a key. What's it open?" Clay asked.

"It's a key to the transportation building," Justin said.

"How'd you get that?"

"I was in the office and found it. I completely forgot that I had it in my pocket the night I got bit by the snake."

"You should take it back to the building. I'm sure they're missing it," Clay said.

"I can't do that, Clay."

"Why not?"

"Trust me, you don't want to know."

"Then what are you going to do with the key, Justin?"

"Nothing right now. I'll keep it in the desk drawer until I decide what to do with it."

"It's not something that will get me into trouble, is it?" Clay asked.

"No, besides, I'll take care of it soon. I just need a day or two."

CHAPTER 10
A LETTER FROM RISA

Justin and Clay woke up the next morning, got dressed and started out the door for breakfast. That's when they saw the note stuffed partway underneath the door. Justin picked up the note, put it in his pocket and continued down the hall, down the stairs and out the front door.

Outside and away from others' ears, he stopped Clay and said, "The note is from Risa. I can tell by her writing on the outside of the envelope. I need to read it. You go ahead to breakfast, and I'll meet you there soon."

Clay walked off toward the cafeteria. Justin headed toward an area near the fountain that was away from prying eyes. There he pulled out the letter from his pocket and read it.

Justin,

You are in danger. You need to leave school. Go back home. You'll be safe there as long as you don't tell anyone what you know.

Please don't worry about me. I am fine. I went back home for a few days. I'm back in Branson now. I'm safe. Please don't come looking for me. I love you, Justin, but it is best for both of us that we don't see each other again. It's too dangerous for both of us.

I'm afraid that Richard is involved in something. He won't talk to me about it. He insists that I am safe as long as I stay with him and don't talk with you. He has some very scary people that he is involved with. I overheard them talking about you.

You don't know how much danger you're in. They are watching you. They are listening to you. You won't be safe as long as you're on campus. Justin, you can't trust anyone. They know everything.

Destroy this letter as soon as you read it.

Goodbye,

Risa.

Justin read the letter a second time. Afterward, he tore it up into small pieces and threw it in the pond. Then he walked to the cafeteria, trying to make sense of what Risa had written on his way.

Was she being held by Richard? Was she in danger? Did she know what Richard was involved in? Did she know who was watching me? he asked himself.

Justin wasn't sure who he could trust. He wasn't sure who had planted the listening device in his dormitory room. He wasn't sure who was involved other than Richard and Karl Gholson in the drug business. He wasn't sure who was following him. He wasn't sure if Risa was involved.

There was one thing that he was certain about. He sure as hell wasn't going to run.

When he met up with Clay in the dining hall for dinner that evening, he told him about Risa's letter.

"You know Clay, if I'm in danger, so are you. I wouldn't blame you if you left school and went back home," Justin said.

"Buddy, if you're staying here, I am too. I've never run from a fight, and I don't intend to now," Clay replied. "Besides, I think that you're going to need someone to watch your back. You seem to be running a little short on friends these days.

By the way, Justin, Earl Myers stopped me on my way from World Lit class earlier today. He told me that he wants to talk to you. He asked that you meet him by the fountain at 9:30 tonight."

"Did he say what he wanted?"

"No, it was a short conversation. I don't think he wanted anyone to see that he was talking to me," Clay said. "Justin, have you been back to our room since this morning?"

"No, have you?" Justin asked.

"No, I feel a little uncomfortable being in there by myself when I know the room is bugged."

"Aren't you curious about the key?" Justin asked.

"Of course, I am. But I was hoping we could both go into the room at the same time."

"Well, let's go now. But if the key is missing, I don't think we should say anything. I think it is better that whoever is listening to us doesn't find out that we know that the key is gone."

"I agree."

A few minutes later, Justin and Clay arrived back at Rowlison Hall. When they entered their room, nothing seemed out of place. Everything seemed exactly the way they left it early that day. They walked inside and turned the radio on to drown out any conversation they might have. Then Justin went to the desk drawer, opened it and looked inside. The key was gone. Justin closed the desk drawer and nodded to Clay.

At 9:20pm, Justin walked out of his room, closing the door softly so as not to be heard and walked toward the pond. He took the long way through the woods behind the dormitory so as not to be seen. Every so often, he stopped, listened for footsteps and glanced around him to see if he was being followed.

It was a chilly, cloudy evening. Few students were outside. Justin was confident that no one had followed him. When he got to the pond, he scanned the area for any people. S of O's pond, about two acres in diameter, was too large to see completely around it. He had no idea where Earl intended to meet him. He stayed close to the tree line, hoping to spot him, but he didn't.

There was no one around.

It was 9:40 when Justin decided to make his way to one of the many benches that lined the area next to the pond. He sat and waited for another ten minutes. After waiting nearly half an hour, Justin walked back to Rowlison Hall. Clay was waiting outside for him.

"What did he say to you, Justin?"

"He didn't. He never showed up."

"That's weird," Clay replied.

"Why'd you leave the room, Clay? They'll know that we both left."

"No, they won't. I turned the volume of the radio up and was careful to make sure no one saw me leave."

It was the Friday before Thanksgiving break that Sheriff Roscoe Dale and two State police officers showed up on campus to talk to Coach Moffit, Karl Gholson and members of the cross-country team. A car had gone off the road near Outlook Mountain. It tumbled down a steep hill, rolled over several times and exploded in flames. Three bodies were found in the car. The car belonged to Earl Myers. He was thought to be one of the bodies in the car. The other two were speculated to be Dennis and Bobby. The bodies were too badly burned for immediate identification, but wallets and other identifiable evidence were found at the scene to point to those three individuals being the victims.

Earl had not been seen on campus since the evening he was supposed to meet with Justin at the pond. Speculation was that Earl, Bobby and Dennis left campus in Earl's car that night and stopped by a liquor store soon after. The fire had charred the remains. The deceased were impossible to identify. The police would need to use dental records to identify the people killed. That would take some time.

The other rumor going around campus was that the driver

of the car was drunk. Beer cans and a bottle of whiskey were found in and around the car.

If that rumor is true, then the person driving the car couldn't be Earl, Justin thought.

Earl liked to party. Justin knew that, but he also knew that Earl was a dedicated athlete. He would never drink during cross-country season. Nationals were coming up in two weeks. Earl had qualified. It was a dream for him to go to the NAIA Nationals.

There was no way he would party before that race, Justin thought. *In fact, there was no way any three of my ex-teammates would go out partying before the season was over.*

One thing was certain, though. Earl was not on campus. Neither was Bobby or Dennis. They did not come back to Brown Hall, show up at classes or attend practice, Justin found out. No one had seen them, and no one knew where they were. Earl Myers, Bobby Cockran and Dennis Glenn were gone.

If they were killed, Justin thought, *then I am the only one left that had broken into the transportation building. Maybe Risa was right. Maybe my life is in danger.*

Justin had his last class before Thanksgiving break the following Tuesday. He packed his bags to go home for five days. He missed his family, and he needed to get away from whatever was going on at S of O. Clay wasn't as lucky. He was assigned to work on Thanksgiving weekend, so he stayed on campus.

"I'll miss you, buddy," Clay told him. "It's just going to be me and whoever is listening in to me this weekend. Maybe, I'll do a little singing in the room to keep them entertained."

"You take care, Clay. Don't get into any trouble."

"I'll be fine. I've got a case of Budweiser cooling outside the window and a cafeteria full of food."

They shook hands, and Justin left and walked up the hill to the student parking lot. Most of the students had already left campus. About three dozen remained to keep the essential operations of S of O going during the break. All the students that stayed had volunteered, including Clay. Most needed the extra money the school paid for those that stayed and worked during the holidays. Some, like Clay, volunteered because campus life was better than their life back home.

When Justin reached the student parking lot, only a handful of cars remained. His red Volkswagen beetle sat alone in one corner of the lot. He unlocked the door and got inside. Lying next to the stick shift was a folded piece of paper. Justin picked it up and unfolded it. It was a note.

Justin,
Don't come back to campus after the break. They will be waiting for you. The same thing that happened to Earl, Bobby and Dennis will happen to you. I love you, Justin. Please don't come back. It's not safe for you anymore.
Risa

Justin folded the note, put it in his pocket, started the engine and drove away. He didn't know if Risa was trying to warn him or if it was a threat. He wasn't even sure if the note was Risa's idea.

Maybe Richard or someone else put her up to it, he thought. *One thing was certain, though. Risa either knew what happened to the three boys, or whoever forced her to write that note knew what happened to them*, Justin thought.

There was something else too. The note was inside Justin's car. Someone had broken into his car to leave that note. The car doors were locked. There was no sign of forced entry. *But that doesn't necessarily mean anything*, Justin thought. On two occasions, Justin had locked his keys inside the car. He had discovered then that by using a simple wire hanger, he could easily slide the wire between the window and metal and unlatch the door lock. *That's probably how they got inside*, he reasoned.

Then another concern came to his mind. *If someone got into his car, maybe the note wasn't the only thing they left inside.*

When he had driven far outside Branson, he pulled into a park on the edge of Nixa, MO and stopped the car. He turned the radio up and searched the inside of the car. Embedded inside the passenger side air vent was a small listening device. Rather than remove the device, he left it there. *It might be an advantage to know someone was listening to whatever was said in his car*, Justin thought.

The drive to Kansas City took nearly five hours. He stopped twice along the way for gas and to eat. By the time he arrived home, it was dinner time.

The Wade's lived in a middle-class neighborhood in Prairie Village, Kansas, a suburb of Kansas City. Their house was a block from the State line that separated Kansas and Missouri. The family had lived in the three-bedroom, ranch-style house since Justin was a baby.

It was a quiet, comfortable area made up of working-class families that, for the most part, kept to themselves. The Wades knew most of their neighbors but seldom interacted with them more than a glancing smile or a wave of the hand.

Both of Justin's parents had worked. Justin's dad, Ron, worked in a manufacturing plant in the city. He had worked there since he got out of the Air Force. He was home now, recovering from a mild stroke. He took the job at Bendix six months before he married his high school sweetheart, Jane. They were married less than a year when Justin was born. For several years, Jane stayed home to take care of her son. Money was tight, but life was good during the early years of their marriage.

Two years after Justin was born, Jane discovered she was pregnant again. This time, it was a difficult pregnancy. She went into labor in her seventh month. Brian, Justin's only sibling, was born pre-mature. He spent the first month of his life in the hospital. Even after he came home, he had developmental issues that required more doctors. Justin's mother would never be pregnant again.

The medical bills were staggering and put a financial strain on the young parents. When Justin began second grade, his mother started to work. At first, she cleaned homes, trying to keep flexible hours so she could be home with Justin when he got out of school.

A few years later, she took a full-time position as a secretary at a law firm. Justin and Brian became latchkey children.

Still, Jane always took the time to make the family a hot breakfast in the morning and a complete dinner at night. She wouldn't admit it, but Jane was an excellent cook, a bit of a natural gourmet. She made exceptional meals on a small budget, and Ron and the boys rarely missed any of them. Justin's dad loved deserts, and every night, dinner was followed by one of his wife's homemade desserts. Apple Pie was Justin's dad's favorite, and every Saturday night, Jane made one.

Justin's home life was good, filled with great childhood memories. He never saw his parents argue. They weren't overly affectionate people, but Justin knew they loved each other deeply.

The Wades were private people. They didn't socialize. They rarely went out as a couple. They felt most comfortable together. Their life was simple, but it was good.

Jane ran out to greet her son when his red Volkswagen pulled into the driveway.

"I missed you, sweetie," she said, throwing her arms around him as soon as he got out of the car.

Justin's mother had always been emotional. She was not afraid to show her feelings. That was the opposite of Justin's dad. He always seemed colder, more distant. He had never been one to show his emotions. Justin had never even heard him say, "I love you."

But still, Justin knew how much his father cared for him, his brother and Jane. Justin's mother used to call him a "tootsie roll pop" because he was hard on the outside but soft inside. He had served in Vietnam for four years. He had been a pilot in the Air Force. Near the end of the war, he was shot down on a mission over North Vietnam. He had been captured and spent nearly a year in a POW camp before escaping. Justin had found that out from his mother. He never talked about the war.

Justin always assumed that his time in captivity taught him to live within himself. He still did that today. He was a quiet, strong man, a proud man that never asked for help or showed his emotions. Still, Justin knew that he would always be there for him and his mother.

"Stop kissing me, mom," it's embarrassing.

"Sorry, honey, I just missed you."

"You just saw me two weeks ago."

"Yes, but a mother never stops worrying about her boy. How was the drive?"

"Long, but it was good."

"How long are you going to be home?"

"I need to go back Sunday after church."

"Justin, a coach from Missouri Western, called earlier today. He wants to talk to you about going there. He said that he might have a scholarship for you. He asked for you to call him. You know Justin, Missouri Western is only an hour away. Your father and I could visit you more often, and you could come home any weekend you wanted."

"Yes, mom. I'll give him a call."

"Guess what I made you for dinner? Smiling, she didn't skip a beat. "Spaghetti and Meatballs, your favorite and cherry pie for dessert."

"Great, thanks, mom."

"And tomorrow we'll have our thanksgiving dinner,

a little earlier than normal, about 2pm, because we're going to have company."

"Who, mom?"

"Elise. Don't give me that look," Jane said to her son. "She's a wonderful girl. Besides, she wanted to come. She misses you, Justin."

"How do you know that, mom?" he asked.

"I can tell it in her voice. She was excited to come. She asked about you."

"Geez, mom. She made it pretty clear when she broke up with me that she wanted to see other guys."

"Maybe she discovered that she was wrong, that you're the one she really cares about. A girl is entitled to make a mistake, you know."

"I know, mom. Just don't get your hopes up. Elise and I are a lot different."

"Not anymore different than your father and me, and look how long we've been married," Jane said with a smile.

"Yeah, well, I've never quite figured that out, mom. You two don't hug or kiss or show any affection toward each other. It just seems odd that you say how much you are in love with each other."

"Your father isn't much for showing his emotions, but I know how much he loves me and how much he loves you. Your father would do anything for either one of us. He's like a bear on the outside and a big teddy bear on the inside. He's been worried about you, you know."

"How do you know that, mom?"

"Look up at the porch to the window in the dining room. Don't be obvious, though. See, the curtain opened just slightly on one side. It's your father watching us. He doesn't want you to know that he's looking, but he's missed you. He's happy that you're home. Your father was up almost all-night last night. He was excited that you were coming home for Thanksgiving, so much so that he had trouble sleeping.

"It was your father's idea that I call Elise and invite her to Thanksgiving dinner. He sees a lot of you in him and a lot of Elise in me. I guess he figured you two would never get back together without a little pushing."

"Where's Brian, Mom?"

"He's probably in his room. He's acting like a typical pre-teen these days, always in his room, not wanting to spend time with his parents. You know how that is. You were just like him at that age."

"No way, mom. I was a lot cooler than he is."

Jane laughed.

When Justin entered the house, his father was sitting in his recliner in the family room reading the newspaper.

"Hi, son," his dad said, looking up from the paper.

"Hi, dad. How are you doing?"

"Just fine. The Chiefs play the Broncos Sunday," he said. "Are you going to be able to watch the game with me?"

"I'd like to, dad, but I need to get back to campus. Maybe we can watch the first half together."

"Yeah, well, if you have time, that would be nice," he said, turning back to read the newspaper.

Ron Wade was a man of few words. People didn't know him, and that was because just about everyone shied away from him. His 6'2", 250lb frame looked intimidating. His inability to smile around strangers made him look gruff and somewhat angry.

But Justin had seen the softer side of his father. He had seen his father make it to every one of his cross-country and track events. He had been there cheering him on. He had seen his father cry, on occasion, once when his mother passed away and once at the funeral of a close war buddy.

"Hey, ugly, how's school?" he heard Brian shout out as he came from his room.

"It's fine, dipstick," Justin snapped back jokingly.

They both missed each other, but they wouldn't dare let the other know it.

That night the family enjoyed dinner together, watched a movie and got caught up on each other's lives.

"Bro, I had my first date two weeks ago," Brian said with a smile.

"What do you mean? You're twelve years old, bro. You're too young to date."

"Well, I'll turn thirteen next month. Besides, the school had a dance, and a girl asked me to it. I couldn't disappoint her."

"You're so full of crap, Brian. What did you pay the girl to go out with you?"

"Funny, bro. Just because I've got all the Wade charm doesn't mean you need to be jealous about it."

"Yeah, you've got about as much charm as dad does, you little creep."

"Hey, wait a second, Justin," his mother said. "Your father has plenty of charm. Just last week, we went to a restaurant to celebrate our anniversary, and your father pulled out the chair for me to sit down."

"Did he wait until you fell down before he pushed the chair back in?" Justin said with a laugh.

Thanksgiving was a wonderful time in the Wade house. Justin's mother got up early to prepare the turkey and put it into the oven. She started her pies while Justin, Brian and their father went downtown to the Thanksgiving Day parade. They had gone every year since Justin could remember. Jane made popcorn for the three of them to eat during the parade.

Justin always suspected that it was his mother's idea for the three of them to go to the parade. It left her alone in the house to make dinner without interruption.

The parade lasted most of the morning, and by the time they got back, it was time to get dressed for Thanksgiving dinner. The Wade men would wear their Sunday best suits, dress shirts, ties and polished shoes. It had always been a tradition for everyone to dress up for Thanksgiving dinner even though, in recent years, they had no other guests for dinner.

Justin could still remember the years when both sets of grandparents came to dinner. But, when he was six years old, his grandmother Rose, Ron's mother, passed away. Less than a year later, Ron's father, Roy, passed on.

And five years ago, both of Jane's parents were killed in a car accident. They were hit by a drunk driver. Their deaths were very difficult on Justin's mother. She was depressed for a long time. When she came out of her depression, she was filled with anger. She refused to allow alcohol in the house anymore. She refused to be around anyone that drank. Ron, out of love for his wife, gave up drinking. He hadn't touched a drink since his in-laws were killed.

Thanksgiving's past that saw wine flow in the Wade house were over. Chardonnay and Burgundy were replaced with iced tea, coffee and soft drinks.

Justin had just finished getting dressed when the phone rang. His mother answered. A few minutes later, she yelled for Justin to come into the kitchen.

"That was Elise on the phone, sweetie. She's having car trouble. Would you mind picking her up?"

"Sure, mom. But could I use dad's car? I'm low on gas."

Justin was low on gas, but that wasn't the reason he wanted to borrow his parent's car. He didn't want whoever planted the listening device in his car to listen to his conversation with Elise.

"Sure, son. But, be careful."

A few minutes later, he left the house to go get Elise. He

hadn't seen her since summer, and he was excited to see her again. Based on their last conversation, he wasn't certain he would ever see her again. He still wasn't certain what her motivation was in accepting his mother's invitation to Thanksgiving dinner.

Did she still have feelings for him? he wondered. *Or is she coming out of friendship?*

Elise and his mother had always gotten along well. She had never said so, but Justin had thought that his mother thought Elise would make a good wife for Justin. Inviting Elise to Thanksgiving dinner had been his mother's idea.

Was she trying to play matchmaker? Justin wondered.

Elise's father was a captain on the Kansas City police force. He reminded Justin of his own father, with a tough exterior and a good heart inside. Justin had met Elise's father before he was able to go on his first date with her. That was her father's rule. He had to meet eye-to-eye with Justin before he would allow her to go out with him. Justin was so nervous about meeting her father, but everything went great. Her father set him at ease right away. He cared deeply for his daughter and just wanted to know that the boy she was dating was well-grounded with a strong moral compass.

Elise's mother was a teacher. She reminded Justin of his own mother. She was a wonderful cook and had a heart of gold, just like his mother.

Elise got her good looks from her mother. She was a beautiful woman at forty-five. The Bacilli family was of Italian descent. Both Elise and her mother had beautifully tanned skin, dark hair and olive eyes. Elise was beautiful.

Justin often wondered what she saw in him. Three days before his high school graduation, the school opened the gymnasium for all the seniors to get together one last time before graduation and get their yearbooks signed. Justin brought Elise with him that day. His friends couldn't believe what a strikingly beautiful woman Justin was with. Throughout high school, Justin had been a fairly quiet, introverted student. His friends were mainly teammates on the cross-country and track teams. They had rarely seen him interact with girls, let alone date one as beautiful as Elise.

That day in the gym, holding Elise's hand and seeing the looks on his friend's faces left him feeling fantastic. What no one knew was that Elise didn't intend to continue her relationship with Justin. That would be his last date with her.

But now, maybe he would have a second chance with her. He was hopeful that he would, but then again, he hadn't even talked to her in nearly six months. He had no idea if she still had feelings for him.

The drive to Elise's house took about thirty minutes. They lived in a modest ranch-style home in the South Kansas City area. The area she lived in was nice. The homes were modest, but the yards were well-maintained. It was the Italian section of town. Many areas around them had seen better days, but their neighborhood looked like a picturesque suburb. The houses were all similar, brick, ranch-style homes with one-car garages. The landscaping was meticulous. Every house looked like they had hired a professional landscape company.

Elise lived in a cul-de-sac, one block from a large park and three blocks from Center High School, where Elise would graduate the following May.

Justin pulled into the Bacilli's driveway just behind the unmarked patrol car that Elise's father drove. He glanced in the rear-view mirror to make sure he looked OK, then he popped a mint in his mouth and got out of the car. He walked up to the front door, took a deep breath and rang the doorbell.

"I'll get it, mom," he heard Elise yell.

The door opened, and Elise held out her arms for a hug.

She is so beautiful, Justin thought to himself.

She was wearing a pink dress with spaghetti straps. The dress was cut just above her knees, showing her gorgeous, long, dark, slender legs. She was wearing pink lipstick that went perfectly with her dress and her dark complexion. Her smile was large, and her eyes were tender.

"A woman's eyes are the window to her soul," his mother once told him.

If that was true, Elise's soul was loving and caring.

"I missed you so much, Justin," she said, looking up at him.

Elise had a tiny frame, maybe five foot tall at the most, thin and small-boned. She was wearing high heels, which maybe added three inches to her height, but still, she needed to lean up to kiss Justin.

"Come on in. Mom and dad want to say hi," she said.

Elise's parents were just a few steps behind her.

"Hello, Justin. It's good to see you again," her mother said with a smile.

"Thank you, Mrs. Bacilli. It's good to see you again too."

"Well, Justin, how's college?" her father said, holding out his hand for Justin to shake.

"It's good, sir, but I sure do miss home."

"Well, why don't you come in and visit for a while," Elise's mother said.

"Mom, we need to go. Mrs. Wade said dinner would be at 2pm. We need to go right away, so we're not late."

"Maybe, we can visit later when I bring Elise home," Justin said.

"That would be nice. I'll save some pumpkin pie for you," Mrs. Bacilli said.

A few minutes later, Justin pulled out of the driveway and started home. He moved his right hand to Elise's lap, slowly, gently, hoping she would react positively. She turned to him and smiled. Then she took her left hand and put it on top of his, gently squeezing it. Justin smiled back at her.

"I missed you, Elise," he said.

"I missed you too, Justin. I am sorry about the way things ended between us just before you went off to school. I didn't want to hurt you. I thought that I was doing what was best for both of us."

"And do you still feel that way, Elise?"

"I don't know how I feel now, Justin. I know that I care deeply for you. I know that I have missed you terribly. I know that I am happiest when you are with me. But I don't know if we have a future together. You're away at college, and next year I'll be going to college too. We'll probably be even farther apart than we are now. I just don't know how any long-distance relationship can work."

"I don't either, Elise. But I know that I want to try."

Her handed tightened around his, and she smiled. *That is a good sign*, Justin thought.

When he came to a stop sign a few blocks away from his home, Justin glanced around to see if another car was around. When he didn't see one, he reached over, put his arm around Elise, and gave her a long, slow kiss. *God, I miss kissing her*, he thought. *Her lips are so soft and tender*. He pulled away from her and started to move the car when he heard the fire trucks. They were speeding up behind him, their lights flashing and sirens on full blast. One, two, then a third fire truck speeded past him, followed closely behind by an ambulance and three police cars.

"It must be a terrible fire," Elise said.

"Yeah," Justin replied.

As he got closer to home, he could see the flashing lights. When he started to turn onto his block, he saw the smoke. Then, he saw the police barricade.

"Stop," a policeman yelled at him.

"What happened, officer?" Justin asked.

"Do you live on this block, son?"

"Yes, sir, 411 Bach."

The policeman's demeanor changed. He spoke more softly.

"Perhaps you better come with me," he said.

CHAPTER 11
A FAMILY IN MOURNING

Jane Wade needed a few ingredients for her Thanksgiving dinner. Justin had borrowed his father's car to pick up Elise. "Honey, would you mind taking Justin's car and picking up a few items at the grocery store?" she asked her husband.

"Sure, Jane. I hope it's got enough gas to get me there and back."

He took the grocery list that his wife had made for him, grabbed Justin's car keys from the desk near the kitchen, gave his wife a quick kiss and headed out the door.

Ron Wade opened the car door, put his seat belt on and turned the ignition.

The explosion shook the entire neighborhood. It rattled the kitchen with such force it knocked Jane to the ground. She picked herself up and ran out the front door. The flames had engulfed the car and set fire to the surrounding bushes. The explosion had sent pieces of the car through the garage door and the front side of the house.

She screamed for her husband. "Ron, oh my God, Ron."

The heat and flames were too much for her to be able to get any closer.

Ron's charred body was removed from the car after the

fire department extinguished the blaze.

His grief-stricken wife was taken to the hospital. She had cuts and bruises, but otherwise, physically, she was fine.

Brian had been in his room. The blast shook him from his bed but otherwise, he wasn't hurt. He ran out the front door to see the flames of his brother's car. He didn't know that his father was inside. But, from the screams of his mother, he knew someone was in the car. His mother was on the ground sobbing uncontrollably. He did his best to console her. It was no use.

Mentally, she was in shock.

The bomb, Justin figured, had been meant for him. Had he taken his car to pick up Elise that day, Justin would have been the one killed. Had his mother not asked her husband to pick up items at the store that day, he would not have been killed.

Both Jane and Justin felt enormous guilt over Ron Wade's death. When the guilt softened, they felt anger.

The FBI investigated the bombing. Justin told them everything. He told them about the meth lab that he had discovered off campus. He told them about the bus trip and how he suspected the school was transporting drugs and receiving payment on certain trips. He told them about the two boys whose bodies had surfaced in the pond. He told them about Karl Gholson, and he told them about Richard. He told them about his teammates that were with him that night in the transportation building. He told them about the car accident that claimed the lives of all three of them. He told them about Risa, and why he suspected she was being held against her will.

They listened intently. They recorded the entire conversation. They said that they would investigate. Then they left.

Justin made most of his father's funeral arrangements. His mother was too distraught. Ron Wade was buried three days later. Jane had the funeral service at Zion Lutheran Church, where the family were members of the congregation. The casket was closed. What remained of her husband's body was so badly charred that she was never able to see him to say goodbye.

From the period of his father's death to the day of his funeral, Dennis remained quiet, calm and stayed pretty much to himself. He hadn't even shed a tear. But the sight of the casket and the solemnness of the funeral service brought all his emotion out.

Justin comforted his brother that day. It was the first time they had ever cried together.

Elise, her father and her mother, were at the funeral. After the burial, Michael Bacilli, Elise's father, walked up to Jane and Justin to give condolences.

"I'm so sorry for your loss, Mrs. Wade. I never met your husband, but my daughter has said so many wonderful things about him that I felt like I knew him. If there is anything we can do for you or Justin, please don't hesitate to call."

"I will, Mr. Bacilli and thank you for your kind words."

"Mrs. Wade, may I speak to Justin for just a minute."

"Yes, of course. I'll wait for you in the car, honey," she said to Justin.

When she walked away, Captain Bacilli spoke to Justin. "Justin, listen to me, son. You need to move your mother and brother out of that house to someplace safe. Use a fake name. Don't tell anyone where you are moving. Don't leave a forwarding address. Do it right away, OK?"

"Do you think they're in danger?"

"I think you're the one in danger, son. But if they can't get to you, they might try to get to your mother and brother."

"What about the FBI? Are they going to do something?"

"I don't know, Justin. I have a friend in the Kansas Bureau. He says they think the mob was involved in your father's murder. But right now, it is too early in their investigation to know what direction it might take.

"Justin, the FBI moves cautiously. They follow every lead, but it takes time. I'm worried that you may not have that much time before they try to come after you again. That meth lab you stumbled onto must be the tip of the iceberg. You've pissed off some dangerous people. I want you, Brian and your mother to go into hiding until this thing gets resolved."

"What about the FBI? Can't they put us into witness protection or hide us some way?"

"They could, but they probably won't, not now anyway. They don't feel your family is in danger now, that whoever was responsible wouldn't dare try again now that the FBI is involved."

"But you don't feel that way, Mr. Bacilli?"

"Let's just say that I would feel more comfortable if the people responsible were caught.

I'm sorry, Justin. But I don't think you can count on the FBI to protect your family right now. But I will help. I want your family to move into a safe house we have in Kansas City. There, we will protect you. Tomorrow, I want you to drive your mother and brother to my house. Don't pack anything. Don't tell her that she won't be coming back. Tell her we are having a small memorial service for your father at our house. When you arrive, a car will take you to the safe house."

"OK, but are you sure this is necessary?"

"Yes. Trust me. If the mob is involved, there is likely a contract on your life. You need protection."

The next day, Justin drove to the Bacilli home. Parked on the street in front of their house was a navy-blue Chrysler. Two men stepped out and got into Justin's father's car. Two other men escorted Justin, Brian and his mother to the Chrysler.

"What's going on?" Jane asked.

"It's OK, Mrs. Wade," one of the men said. "We're taking you somewhere that you'll be safe."

The two men that got into Ron Wade's car drove back to the Wade's home. They pulled the car into the garage, got into another car that was following behind them and left.

The car that the Wades were in went on the highway toward the southern suburbs of Kansas City. Near Grandview, MO, the car exited the highway and drove down several side streets and into three residential neighborhoods before stopping in the driveway of a modest ranch-style home.

Jane and her sons got out of the car and went inside. There, two different plain-clothed officers were waiting.

"Please, Mrs. Wade, make yourselves at home," one of the officers said. "Two officers will be with you at all times during your stay here. Anything, clothes, food, medicine, we will get for you. For your safety, none of you is to leave this house for any reason. We have provided you clothes and toiletries. If we missed anything, just let us know, and we'll get it for you. The curtains are to remain closed, and the doors locked at all times. Do you understand?"

All three nodded.

The three were prisoners in a strange home. Jane Wade, who was already depressed from the loss of her husband, sank deeper into depression. There were many days that she rarely got out of bed. She stopped eating. She was becoming fragile.

Justin tried to keep his mother's spirits up. He spent hours by her bed, reading to her, talking to her, but nothing seemed to snap her out of it. The doctor prescribed antidepressant medication. It seemed to help, but it made her tired.

Mom has given up, Justin reasoned.

On occasion, Captain Bacilli would visit, always by himself. "It is unsafe for Elise or anyone you care about to know where you are," he would say. But he always brought a letter from Elise.

"She wrote this for you," her father would say. "I can't tell her where you are. I can only tell her that you are safe."

Justin took the letter from her father. He put it in his pocket and would read it at night before he went to bed. That was the hardest part of the day for him. It was the time he was most alone with his thoughts. Elise's letters helped.

"Can you tell Elise that I miss her, Mr. Bacilli?"

"You know that I can't do that, Justin. She mustn't know that I know where you are hiding. It wouldn't be safe for her or our family. But I can tell you, with every bit of certainty, that she knows that you miss her, and she misses you too. You know, at night, when she goes to bed, I hear her praying for you and your mother. I have heard her cries. Elise cares deeply for you, Justin, and she would tell you that if she could."

"Thank you, Mr. Bacilli," he said, wiping a tear from his eye.

That night, just before bedtime, he opened Elise's letter and read it.

> Justin,
> I miss you so much. I can't imagine what you are going through. My father tells me that you are safe. That's all that he will say. I don't even know if you are getting my letters, but I have to hope that you are. Know that when all this is over, I will be waiting for you. Tell your mother that I am praying for her, and I'm praying for you and your brother too, Justin. They say that sometimes a person doesn't really know what they want until they almost lose it. Well, that is the case with me. Come back to me, Justin. I promise that I will never hurt you again.
> Love,
> Elise

Some people never find love, Justin thought. *Some only find it once in a lifetime. I had found love twice that year.*

But, with Elise, the love felt natural. It wasn't one-sided.

It wasn't forced. There wasn't someone else competing for that love. Unlike Risa, Justin knew that Elise meant what she said. He knew that she didn't have an alternative motive. Risa had always been a mystery to him. He felt that she loved him. He wanted her to love him. But she always went back to Richard. He was like the "bad boy" that she just couldn't stop loving. With Risa, he would always wonder if he was the safe choice for her but not the person she really loved. With Elise, he knew that she loved him. He knew that he was her first choice.

Elise was the better choice for him. But he still cared deeply for Risa. He needed to know if Risa was with Richard because she loved him or because she feared him. He needed to know if she was in danger. He would need to find out the answer to that. And, if she was in danger, he would do everything he could to rescue her.

Christmas was not a happy time in the Wade house that year. There was no Christmas tree in the Wade house. There were no decorations and no presents under the tree. Justin got up early and put a present under the tree for his brother and one for his mother. He had slipped out of the house earlier that week to buy gifts. Then he made breakfast, scrambled eggs, ham and biscuits.

When Brian woke up, he opened his present and ate breakfast. Justin tried to get his mother to come out to join them for breakfast, but she wouldn't. So, he took the present in to her along with a breakfast plate. Jane didn't get out of bed the entire day. Justin could hear her crying from behind her closed bedroom door. He tried several times to comfort his mother. But she sent him away.

"I just want to be left alone, Justin," she would say.

Justin couldn't help but think that his mother blamed him for the death of his father. After all, it was Justin that was the target of the car bomb. It was Justin that insisted on taking his father's car to pick up Elise. And when one of the FBI agents let it slip to her that her son had discovered the listening device in his car on the trip home from school, she blamed Justin for not notifying the police.

Jane loved her son. She always would, no matter what. But everyone deals with grief differently. She had fallen into depression. Justin assumed his mother had felt guilt for sending her husband to the store that day. Now she was looking to blame someone for his death.

Justin and his brother spent the day watching television and listening to music. They tried to put on a happy face, but it was a terribly sad day. The two policemen that normally stayed in the house with them had gone home to spend Christmas Day with their families. They would be back in a few hours. In the meantime, the police would patrol the neighborhood every so often.

Justin had time to think. He had no idea where the FBI was in their investigation. For all he knew, they hadn't taken his statement as credible. No one from the FBI had talked to him since the day after his dad's funeral.

Justin had to do something. He couldn't just sit around and wait. He had never been an impulsive person, but he would become one that day. Many times, he had blamed himself for his dad's murder. If he had taken his car instead of his dad's, it would have been him killed, not his father. If he had reported the listening device inside his car to the police, maybe his father would be alive today. Inside, Justin felt tremendous guilt. Outside, he felt anger.

That anger festered that Christmas Day. It became overwhelming, all-consuming. It became stronger than his fear for his life.

"Brian, I want you to take care of our mother for a few days. There is something I need to do. You'll be safe here."

"Where are you going, Justin?" Brian said with a concerned

look on his face.

"Don't worry, bro. I'll be fine. I'll be back in a few days, and then I'll tell you all about it."

Justin wrote a note. Put it on the coffee table in the living room and walked out the back door. Two blocks down the road, he found an unlocked car on the street with the keys in a cupholder next to the steering wheel. He got inside, started the engine and drove off. When the officers that were assigned to the house arrived back that evening, they discovered the note. It was addressed to "Mom."

Mom,

I'm so sorry for what has happened. I made a mistake. I should have never put you or dad in danger. It is me they want, not anyone else. I need to take care of this. Please don't worry about me. I'll be careful. I promise that I'll come back when all of this is over.

Love,
Justin

The officers that read the note never gave it to Jane. They were afraid that she might be unable to handle the news that her son had left and was likely going back to Branson. Instead, they told her that the FBI had taken him to put him into protective custody. They told her that she would see her son soon.

Justin drove the stolen car to Springfield. He abandoned it at the Greyhound bus depot. There, he boarded a bus for Branson. By the time he arrived in Branson, it was late. He found a bench in a park overlooking Taneycomo Lake and bedded down there for the night.

The long trip to Branson gave Justin time to formulate his plan. He had no idea if it would work, but he had to try. He had to do something.

***

The day after Christmas, Captain Bacilli took Justin's note

to his friend with the Kansas Bureau of Investigation.

"I think Justin has gone back to Branson. I think that he is going to confront the people that are after him. You need to help him, David. He's going to get himself killed."

"You know, Mike, there is very little that we can do. We can't jeopardize the investigation by going after him."

"No, but you can keep an eye on him. It's very likely that he will get the attention of the people involved in the drug organization. If you are watching Justin, you might catch the people involved in the drug activity down there."

"I can't make you any promises, Mike. But I'll take this to my boss."

"Thanks, David."

***

Justin knew the general area where the condo was located, but he didn't have the address. Risa had told him once that it was a large, three-story condo that overlooked the lake in the Taney Hills subdivision. That's where he waited and watched, trying to get a glimpse of Risa or Richard. He sheltered near the lake during daylight and canvassed the area at night when it was less likely that he would be spotted.

On the third night, he saw Karl Gholson leaving a house. At least, he thought it was Karl. When his car had disappeared through the neighborhood, Justin circled around to the back of the condominium. There were three levels of wooden decks in the back, with stairs on one side leading up to each level. There was a light fog that night coming off the lake. Deck lights were turn on the second and third levels. The lights collided with the fog, causing a glare that made visibility poor. He could hear music and talking coming from the top deck. He couldn't make out the people that were there. They were like silhouettes in the fog and light from the deck light. From their talk, he figured there were six to eight people on the deck, both women and men.

He moved closer to the deck in an attempt to recognize anyone that was there. He hoped that the fog would hide his movements from their view.

But getting closer did not help. As he got closer to the deck, the people on the top deck began to go out of view, hidden behind the guard rails and angled away from his eyesight to the top deck. He decided to wait until the group went inside. The shades were open on the windows. When they were inside, he would move to the deck and look through the windows. But just as he turned to move farther away, he recognized a voice. It was coming from one of the people on the top deck. He would recognize that voice anywhere.

It was Earl Myer's voice.

CHAPTER 12
THE CONDO

Earl's car had been found wrecked at the bottom of a steep hill. Three bodies were inside, burned beyond recognition. It was assumed one of the persons killed in the car accident was Earl Myers.

But after hearing Earl's voice from the top deck of the condominium, Justin knew that someone else's body had been found in Earl's car. *But whose body was it? And what is Earl doing at the condo?* Justin wondered.

Justin backed into the woods behind the condominium, just off the lake. There he waited for the people on the upper deck to go inside. He wanted to get a look inside the condo to see if he could recognize any of the people and to see if Risa was in the condo.

An hour later, the temperature cooled into the forties. A steady rain began to fall. The people on the upper deck began going inside. When Justin could no longer hear anyone outside, he moved toward the condo. Quietly he walked onto the lower-level deck and to the window. The curtain was closed most of the way, but there was enough of an opening to give him a narrow view inside. The lower level contained a billiard table and a bar. There were four men at the bar. They were young men, maybe in their late twenties or early thirties. They were well dressed in slacks, polo shirts and sports jackets. None looked young enough to be college students. Justin didn't recognize any of them.

After watching for a few minutes, Justin climbed the stairs to the second level. Through the window, he could make out a bedroom. The lights were off, but the door was open, and a hall light shined into the bedroom, illuminating it just enough for Justin to see that no one was in it.

It was on the upper deck, the third level of the condominium, that Justin got his best view of the inside. The entrance to the condo on the third deck was a sliding glass door. The curtains were completely open. Justin could see everything inside. But he had to be careful because the people inside could see outside, also. He peeped in at an angle from the very edge of the sliding glass door. Inside was a large living room and kitchen and what appeared to be more bedrooms.

Then he saw her. Not more than twenty feet away, sitting on a sofa in the living room, was Risa. She showed no signs of being held against her will. She looked happy.

Earl Myers was there too. He was sitting on a stool near the kitchen. Justin also recognized Karl Gholson. He was talking to Earl.

No one in that condo appeared to be there against their will, at least for the people Justin could see. There were at least a half-dozen women, young, maybe college age, none that Justin recognized. None that looked like S of O students. There were other men, older, in their thirties and forties. All were dressed well. They looked like people you would expect to see at a cocktail party or company gathering.

After a few minutes, Justin went back down the stairs and off the decks. He circled to the side of the condo. It was a corner unit, so one side of it was exposed from the outside. It connected to four other condominiums; each were three-story townhomes. Each with three decks facing out to the lake.

On the side of the condo were two windows, each a few

inches higher than ground level. Both had curtains covering the windows. He pushed up on each, but they were both locked from the inside. Justin reached into his pocket and pulled out a switchblade knife he had taken from his house before he left. It was a knife he had used when he went camping with his father when he was younger. His father had shown him once when he had locked himself out of the house when returning from a camping trip how to slide the knife's blade between the window and frame and wiggle the window latch open.

So, Justin gave it a try.

It isn't as easy as Dad made it seem, he thought.

It took him nearly fifteen minutes to reach the latch and ten more minutes to unlock it.

He pulled the window up slightly, enough to move the curtain slightly to look inside. It was completely dark inside. He couldn't see a thing. He opened the window farther and crawled inside backward to allow his legs to dangle down to the floor. It was about a four-foot drop to the basement floor. His feet make a loud noise as they hit the concrete floor. His heart raced, fearful that if anyone was in the basement, they would hear the noise.

He stood motionless for a few seconds waiting for any sound of someone coming. Confident that no one heard him, he moved farther into the basement. When his eyes had adjusted somewhat to the dark, he followed the walls of the basement. As he went, he opened the drapes to both windows to provide some light from the street and deck lights outside.

The basement was cold and bare, with concrete walls, concrete floors and only a few boxes piled on a storage shelf against the inner wall. The ceiling was made of wood beams stretching from one end to the other. Thick pads of foam insulation occupied the spaces between the wood beams. There were two lights installed in the ceiling, both single light bulbs with long pull cords dangling from them.

There was one thing that struck Justin as odd about that ceiling. The pads of insulation dangled much lower than the beams of the ceiling. It was unusually thick, thick enough to deaden sound. At the far side of the basement, the side closest to the back of the condo and the decks, the ceiling was lowered about five feet, creating an open crawl space. Justin walked slowly to that space to examine it a little better. The crawl space was about twelve feet wide, extending from the inner basement wall to the outer wall. The concrete floor going into the crawl space appeared to be newer than the rest of the basement floor. It was darker and of a different texture than the rest of the basement floor. It also flowed downward at an angle, not a steep angle but one that appeared to drop about four feet over the course of a few yards.

Justin figured the crawl space went underneath the lower deck in the back yard. He decided to crawl in to explore what its purpose was. It was completely dark inside. He crawled down for about five yards, and then the floor leveled out. The ceiling appeared to be made of concrete. So were the walls on either side. It reminded Justin of the drain tunnels he and his friends used to crawl through when he was younger. They were fun to explore.

Another five yards or so after the floor leveled out, Justin came upon the outer wall, also made of concrete. That's when he found the door. Almost exactly in the middle of the outer wall was a wooden door with a lock on the outside. He pulled on the lock, hoping it was not fully engaged. But it was. The lock was thick and well-secured. He took the small blade of his knife and tried to fit it into a small hole located next to the lock mechanism.

One time, Justin picked a lock on his school locker by inserting the end of a wire into the same type of hole and twisting it. But the knife blade was too wide to fit in the hole. He searched his pockets, hoping to find something that would fit into the hole. But he had nothing that would work.

That's when he heard the noise coming from the other side of the door. It was faint. He could barely make out the word, "Help!"

He moved out of the crawl space and back into the basement, hoping to find something to help him open the lock. Someone was being held in that hidden room, and he had to find out who it was.

He went to the shelf near the back of the basement and rummaged through the boxes, looking for anything that might help him get into that room.

That's when he heard the basement door open and then close. He ducked down behind several of the boxes hoping not to be seen. A light came on. He heard footsteps coming down the stairs. From his hiding place, Justin could not see the person coming into the basement.

It was a man, he assumed, from the sound of heavy footsteps. Justin could see the shadow of the person bend down and move into the crawl space. Then he heard the sound of the lock being moved and then the door opening.

He grabbed a hammer he found in a toolbox on the shelf and moved quickly but quietly to the crawl space. The door was open at the end of the crawl space, and a light was shining through, illuminating much of the area.

Justin moved into the crawl space and toward the hidden room, staying as close to the inner wall as possible so as to remain in the shadows. When he reached the door, he could hear the man talking to someone inside.

"Time for your medication to put you to sleep. Tomorrow, we're going to move you," Justin could hear him say.

Soon after, he heard what sounded like a cage door shut and a lock being engaged. Justin backed slowly away from the door, still hugging the wall in an effort to avoid being seen. The light in the room went out, and he heard the man start to exit the room. Justin raised the hammer. When the man turned his back to lock the door, Justin attacked, striking the man once in the back of the head. He fell to the ground, face first into the doorway, blocking the entrance into the hidden room.

Justin pulled his body out of the doorway. The hammer had created a deep gash on the back of his head that was bleeding a lot. Justin tore a piece of the person's shirt and tied it tightly around his head to help stop the bleeding. Then, he turned him over.

The man was Richard. He was alive, but the blow had knocked him out.

Justin walked inside the room, felt around for the light switch and when he found it, he flipped the switch on.

"Shit," he hollered.

In a wire cage about the size of a large breed dog kennel was his roommate, Clay.

"Good to see you, buddy," Clay said when he saw Justin standing there.

"What the hell is going on, Clay? Why are they holding you here?"

"I'd love to tell you everything I know, Justin, but I'm afraid we don't have time. They'll be coming down to see why Richard didn't come back real soon. Besides, the medication he gave me works quickly, and in a few minutes, you'll need to carry me out of here."

"Grab the key to the lock, buddy. It's in Richard's front pocket."

Justin found the key and unlocked the cage door. Then he helped Clay out of the cage and through the crawl space to the basement window where he had first entered the basement. He climbed out the window first and pulled Clay out behind him.

It was pouring down rain outside. The fog had thickened, and the moon was buried behind a wall of thick clouds. It was a good night to stay hidden from view.

The two friends ran until the medication that Clay had been given began to take hold. He slowed. His legs began to go numb.

About four blocks away from the condo, Justin found a cabin that appeared that no one was living there, at least this time of year. Many of the homes in the Branson area, particularly around the lake, were summer homes. They were closed in the fall and re-opened again in late spring. The cabin that Justin found appeared to be a seasonal home. He broke through a window and climbed inside. Then he pulled Clay through the open window. The utilities had been turned off, but the cabin provided them shelter from the rain and cold outside.

He dragged Clay to a bedroom and lifted him onto a bed. His clothes were soaked. So were Justin's. In a closet, he found some clothes. They were much larger than either of them wore, but they would do until their clothes had time to dry. Clay was sound asleep. The medication had taken hold of him. Justin removed his friend's wet clothes, hung them up in the bathroom to dry and covered him with blankets he had found in a hall closet.

Then he removed his wet clothes and put on the warm, dry clothes he had found in the closet. He found some canned food in the cabinets, opened two cans with his knife and made a meal of pickled beets and cream corn.

The accommodations were sparse, but there were two bedrooms with beds, bed sheets and blankets. It was more than he had hoped for and would provide him a good night's sleep and some time to develop a plan.

Sleep came easily that night. The rain softened to a gentle mist. The cool temperature outside was conducive to a good night's rest. Justin woke a little past sunrise. He sat at the kitchen table and watched the sun rise over the lake. The sky was blue.

The rain clouds and the fog that accompanied them the night before were gone. It was a gorgeous day, one that was infrequent for an early winter evening in the Ozarks.

Clay woke up about thirty minutes later. He joined Justin at the kitchen table.

"Hey, buddy. Thanks for rescuing me," Clay said. "I think they were going to kill me. What the hell are you doing down here, anyway?"

"They killed my dad, Clay. I think they meant to kill me. I had to do something."

"Shit, I'm sorry to hear that, buddy. So, you came down here to get some revenge?"

"Something like that, Clay."

Justin told Clay everything that had happened since he left for home, including the listening device he found in his car.

"Clay, what happened to you. How did you get in the basement of that condo?"

"Wednesday night, the campus was almost completely empty. Everyone had gone home for the Christmas break. I stayed on campus to work. I really didn't want to go home. They pay triple time during the Christmas break, and the cafeteria is stocked with food. It's really a sweet deal. It was quiet, too quiet for me. I'll tell you. It was a little spooky too. You know, when the Rowlison dorm is empty, that old building makes some really weird noises. I couldn't sleep. I decided that I'd go down to the main floor. I thought, maybe, I could watch some television or something, maybe find something to eat. Most of the lights were out. I think they must have turned a lot of them off to conserve energy while most of the students were away. As I came down the stairs, I could hear voices coming from the main floor. I thought that some of the other guys that were stuck on campus during the break had the same idea that I did and were gathered together watching television.

"But then I heard the scream. It was a terrible scream, a scream that sounded like the person was suffering terrible pain. Then, as suddenly as it happened, it went away. The voices stopped too. When I reached the ground floor, I saw several men carrying someone outside the front door. So, I followed them by staying far enough back that they couldn't see me. There was a campus security car parked outside of the dorm. I saw the men load the person they were carrying into the trunk. Then they got inside the car and drove away. The car did not have its lights, but I could see where it was going because the campus lights were on. It drove in the direction of the pond. When the car was completely out of sight, I walked toward the pond.

"I was careful to avoid the lights, taking the long way around following the tree line. When I got close enough, I could see two men wrapping what looked like a body up in a canvas. They tied a rope around it, and then I saw them weigh it down with what looked like cinder blocks. The lights from the fountain gave me a good view of two men in a rowboat, taking the canvas to the center of the pond, just in front of the fountain. They dropped the canvas just in front of the fountain.

"Justin, I think that I witnessed a murder.

"I ran. I wanted to get to a phone back in the dorm. I had to call the police. I had to tell them what I saw. I made it to the phone, and I called the police. But the only one to arrive was the Branson sheriff. I knew then that I had made a mistake. Whatever is going on, the sheriff is in on it. He handcuffed me, put me in the back of his car and drove me to the condo. They beat the shit out of me that night; they tried to find out exactly what I saw. Then, they wanted to know what else I knew. They wanted to know about you, Justin. They wanted to know what you told me. They knew you were one of the people who broke into the transportation building. They knew that you had found the meth lab. They wanted to know if you had hidden any evidence."

"Who were they, Clay? Did you recognize any of them?"

"Yes, I recognized the head of campus security. I don't know his name, but I've seen him around campus a lot. I also recognized Richard, Karl Gholson and your friend, Earl Myers.

"When I wouldn't talk, they took me into that hidden room in the basement crawl space. They put me in a cage and drugged me. They beat me up more the next day, yesterday. They threatened to kill me and my family. When they told me that they were going to move me today, I figured they were going to kill me and drop me in that pond. I've got to say, I was damn glad to see you show up, buddy.

"Do you have a plan, Justin?"

"Yes, but it's not a safe one. If you want to get out of here, Clay, I've got enough money to get you a bus ticket that will get you back home or someplace else that is safe."

"Buddy, I don't think any place is safe for either of us right now. If they got to you in Kansas City, I'm sure they can find me no matter where I go. I'd just as soon stay with you. Besides, I feel like a little revenge."

"Clay, did you see Risa when you were at the condo?"

"No, I didn't. They had me down in the basement the whole time. The room they kept me in was soundproof. I couldn't hear a thing, and I didn't see anyone except the assholes I told you about."

CHAPTER 13
THE PLAN

When Richard didn't return from the basement, two men went downstairs to check on him. They found him unconscious on the floor in front of the crawl space.

That's when the Sheriff was called. The phone rang a half-dozen times before the Sheriff picked it up. "Damn it, this better be important 'cause you called me right in the middle of a wet dream," he said.

"Sheriff, Clay escaped."

"What the fuck, Karl? Can't you do anything right?"

"I think Justin broke him out. He nearly killed one of my best men to get him out."

"You worthless piece of shit. You were supposed to take care of both of them. What, do I have to do everything for you, Karl?"

"No, we'll find them and take care of it, but I think we're going to need your help. We're going to need to move a lot of merchandise in case they aren't alone. Can you alert us if you hear anything? Also, can you get some of your men to keep an eye on the other side of the lake in case they try to get to our place in the woods?"

"Yeah, I'll take care of it. But when you find them this time, take care of the problem permanently. Do you hear me?"

"Yes, I hear you, Sheriff."

The gash left by the hammer blow left a deep cut in the back of Richard's head. But he was lucky. He would survive with no more than a few stitches and a hell of a headache. Risa stayed with him while most of the others in the condo went searching for Clay and Justin.

"I love you, Richard," she told him, giving him a gentle kiss on the lips. "I'm so sorry for what I did. But I'll never leave you again. When this is all over, let's get married and move back to Sikeston."

Richard didn't say a word. He just smiled and reached for her hand. He had dated Risa since she was a freshman at Sikeston High. He knew her better than anyone. She was so full of love, and she was impulsive. That was a bad combination. She had never been with anyone except Richard until she met Justin. What she saw as a second chance at love was no more than infatuation. Richard always knew that she belonged to him. He knew that she would tire of Justin and come back to him. He knew they were meant to be together. He also knew that her affair with Justin had put her life in danger. He was trying to protect her by keeping her at the condo. She had no idea how close she came to being killed.

Right now, there was nothing he could do to protect anyone. He would need to heal. At least he had Risa by his side to nurse him back.

Only a handful of men remained at the condo. Richard wasn't sure if they were there to keep an eye on Risa or there to wait in case Justin returned. Karl had an idea that Justin might come back for Risa. He was convinced that Justin was in love with her. He was equally convinced that Risa still had feelings for Justin. Earl Myers remained at the condo too. Karl thought he would be useful as bait if Justin were to return. After all, Justin and Earl were good friends. Karl figured that Justin trusted Earl, and he could use that to his advantage.

In ten more days, Christmas break would end, and the students would return to campus. Karl figured that whatever Justin was going to do, he would do before the students came back to campus. He was right.

***

Justin shared his plan with Clay. The two friends waited until nightfall. Then, they left the cabin. About a mile away, in a cove near the lake and hidden away from other homes, they found a pickup truck parked on a gravel road near a house. The doors were unlocked, and inside they found the keys.

"People in the Ozarks never lock anything," Clay said with a smile.

They got inside, started the truck up and took off. Several miles north of Branson, Justin turned down a gravel road and onto a construction site. The state was building a new highway that connected with Highway 65 north of Branson and would bypass Branson on the west to connect with the tourist area of Branson to the west of town. The project was designed to alleviate summer tourist traffic in downtown Branson. The challenge was that mountains surrounded the town on three sides. In order to construct a highway, the state had to blast through miles of mountain rock. The area that Justin drove to was where they stored the dynamite and blasting material to do the job.

The entire complex was fenced in. Normally, the entire area would be illuminated in lights, and there would be guards stationed at the entrance. But no one was there tonight, and the area was completely dark. It was New Year's Eve. Justin reasoned that they were off that weekend and home with their families.

The lock on the gate to enter the area was strong. The fence was at least ten feet high. Justin and Clay considered climbing it, but then they would need to carry everything they needed back to the truck. So, Justin backed up the truck about one hundred feet. "Buckle up," he told Clay. Then he pressed all the way down on the accelerator. He was going about fifty miles an hour when he collided with the gate. It flew open under the force of the truck.

It took only a few minutes for the two friends to find the shed that housed the explosives. The door to the shed was locked, but the wooden building was old and in poor condition. Justin and Clay were able to pry some of the wood planks away from the shed and get inside.

Once inside, they used a flashlight they found in the cabin earlier that day to find the boxes of explosives. They loaded four cases of dynamite, along with blasting caps and fuses into the back of the truck and drove away.

Justin drove to the other side of the lake, down several gravel roads that led to the edge of the lake. There, he parked the truck in a hidden area off the gravel road. Justin and Clay grabbed two cases of dynamite and fuses and began walking through the woods.

It was cold that night, near freezing, the wind was blowing, but the moon was out. There didn't appear to be a cloud in the sky. The moon provided just enough light to move through the dense Ozark woods. The flashlights the boys had taken from the cabin helped guide their way.

When they emerged from the woods onto a path leading to the meth lab, they could see lights in the distance. The closer they got, the brighter the lights were. They heard voices in the distance.

"People are at the lab," Clay said. "Maybe we should wait."

"Let's see what is going on first. Then, we can decide what to do," Justin said.

They got off the path and went into the woods to go around to the side of the property in hopes of getting a better look and avoiding being seen.

Clay was the first to spot the ATVs, eight of them, all near the entrance to the lab. They were being loaded with large canvas bags. One-by-one, as they were loaded, they were driven off in the direction of campus.

"Do you know where they are going?" Clay asked.

"I've got a good idea," Justin said. "When we broke into the transportation building, Dennis found a logbook in a desk drawer. I remember seeing it. It listed dates, cities and bus numbers. For each, there was a code listed. I remember seeing one that seemed out of character from the rest. It was dated January 2. It listed Chicago as the destination, and it listed a bus number, but I can't remember what it was. The code, if I remember correctly, was 20L, 1000 something. I thought a lot about that code. I think it is the number of pounds of meth and the payment. I think they are transporting the meth to the transportation building to be loaded on a bus leaving January 2nd."

"Should we follow them?" Clay asked.

"No, let's see what happens," Justin replied.

After all of the ATVs had left, the lights in the compound were turned off. The area went completely dark. There were no sounds coming from the area. It appeared that everyone had left. But, in complete darkness, it was impossible to know that for sure.

"Time to find out if anyone is watching the lab, Clay," Justin said with a smile. Slowly, they came out of the woods. "If there are sensors surrounding the property, we'll know soon enough," Justin said. "If the lights go on or if an alarm sounds, run back into the woods and head back to the truck."

With each step farther onto the property, they expected the lights to come on. But they didn't.

The sensors around the property must have been turned off, Justin speculated.

That wasn't necessarily good news, Justin thought. There was always a possibility that this was an ambush. *After the break-in at the condo, they might be expecting us.*

They were about fifty yards from the building when Clay saw the flash of what looked like a match lighting a cigarette at the entrance to the building.

"You lay down and stay with the dynamite," Justin whispered to Clay.

Justin moved quietly toward the rear of the building, hoping to come up from behind. As he moved closer, he watched and listened for any sign of people. He heard nothing. Justin circled around to the other side of the building. There was one window on that side of the building. The shades were down on it, and there were no lights on inside. He edged up to the side of the building, hoping that if anyone was inside, they would not see him.

Justin was ten feet from the front door when he heard someone say, "Stop, put your hands up where I can see them and turn around."

Justin did as he was told. When he turned around, a large man wearing a security guard uniform was standing there, pointing a gun directly at him.

"What are you doing here, boy?" he asked. "This is private property. You're in a world of trouble, son," he said. "Turn around and put your hands behind your back," he said, reaching on his belt for a pair of handcuffs.

Then Justin heard a loud crash and saw the guard fall to the ground. Clay was behind him, holding a large, thick branch.

"I couldn't warn you, buddy. The guard out front smoking the cigarette must have seen or heard you. He came in behind you. I figured that I had to do something to save your ass."

Clay bent down and picked up the gun that had fallen to the ground. Then he removed the handcuffs from the guard and put them on him. He reached into the guard's pockets and found a set of keys and a cell phone.

One of the keys opened the front door to the meth lab. Clay was the first to enter, holding the gun. Justin followed. It was completely dark inside. Clay used the flashlight to find a light switch. When he turned it on, the inside looked like a regular cabin with a living room, kitchen, bedroom and bathroom. It certainly didn't appear to be a meth lab.

The boys searched every inch of the main floor. They didn't find anything until they moved a rug underneath the bed in the one bedroom. That's when they saw the trap door with a latch secured by a lock.

One of the keys they had taken from the guard's pocket opened the lock. They removed it and opened the trap door. Beneath it were stairs. It was completely dark inside. Justin took his flashlight and shined it down into the area. At the bottom of the stairs was a large open area with a concrete floor. The area smelled like a hospital room. It was clean and smelled like antiseptic.

Justin and Clay walked down the stairs to the room beneath. The room was completely white, sterile and cold. A ventilation system pumped clean, fresh air into the room and a large air conditioning unit against one wall kept the room cold. The room was reminiscent of a morgue. There was not a spot of dirt or dust anywhere.

The area, about fifteen feet wide and twenty feet long, was completely void of furniture or clutter. At the back end of the room was a narrow hallway.

Justin shined the flashlight along the wall until he found a light switch. Then he turned the lights on. The room illuminated from six large florescent lights attached to the ceiling.

"If anyone is down here, they know they have company now," Clay said, looking at Justin.

Clay raised the gun, and both boys headed into the narrow walkway. Ten feet down the hallway were two steel doors on each side. Both doors were locked.

Clay raised his gun and fired one shot into the lock on the door to his left. The lock blew open. He did the same on the lock attached to the door on the right side of the hallway. Justin opened one door. Clay opened the other.

One room contained dozens of metal shelves stretching from the ground to the ceiling. They were all empty.

The other room contained stainless steel equipment and tables used for cooking and packaging meth. That room was the meth lab. It was easily the largest room, about half the length of a football field and nearly as wide. It was built underground with large ventilation systems and commercial air conditioning unit pumping cool, fresh air into the room.

The meth lab was empty. All supplies, ingredients and product had been removed. The room was completely clean and void of any evidence.

"Damn, they must have known we were coming," Justin said.

"Justin, do you know where they took the drugs?"

"Not for sure, but I have a good idea."

They spent the remainder of the night setting up explosives inside the lab. They ran the fuses through the ventilation system to the outside. Then they moved the fuse to the wooded area behind the building, burying it in the ground as they went. They set up the detonator in the woods about two hundred feet from the building.

"Clay, I need you to stay here. Keep out of sight. When you hear an explosion, push the detonator and blow up the lab. If, for some reason, the explosion doesn't occur by sunrise, go ahead and blow up the lab anyway. Then, get the hell out of here. Take the truck and drive to Kansas City, to Elise's house. Tell her father what has happened and that, most likely, Karl Gholson and Sheriff McClain are holding me or I'm dead. Either way, he'll know what to do."

"Where are you going, buddy?"

"I'm going to find those drugs and blow them up."

"Shit, be careful, Justin."

Justin took the gun and the rest of the explosives and started on foot back to the campus. The only place he could think of where they would keep the drugs was the hidden room in the back of the office of the transportation building.

It is too soon to load them on the bus leaving for Chicago. They would need to store them someplace safe until then, Justin thought. They had stolen the key from Justin and Clay's dormitory room a month earlier. They didn't know that Justin had made a second copy of the key.

It was a long shot that they would hide the drugs in the vault of that hidden room. But it was the only place Justin could think of. Even if the drugs were in that vault and Justin was able to get inside the hidden room, he didn't know the combination to the vault. There was no way that he could get to the drugs.

Justin avoided the path back to campus. Instead, he went through the dense woods in an attempt to avoid detection. It was the long way around to the transportation building, and in the dark, it was a challenging walk. He chose not to use the flashlight he carried. He didn't want anyone to see him coming. The moon, as it peeked out behind the clouds, provided his only light. The woods around him were dense. They provided him with cover.

An hour into his walk, he saw the lights from the lot outside the transportation building. It appeared every light in the parking lot was on.

They are waiting for me, Justin thought. Fifty yards from the edge of the lot, still deep enough in the woods that he couldn't be spotted, Justin set up the first explosives. He buried them next to a large oak tree and attached a fuse. Then he moved fifty yards to the side of the building and buried more explosives.

After that, Justin moved to the path used by the ATVs to transport the drugs from the lab to campus. He buried explosives near several large trees on both sides of the path. He waited there.

The first rays of daylight were beginning to come over the horizon. He had told Clay to blow up the meth lab if he had not heard an explosion by daylight. He hoped that Clay would do as he had told him.

As the sun rose higher over the horizon, Justin waited nervously with thoughts that either the explosives that he and Clay had set did not work or that Clay had chosen not to follow his instructions.

It was nearly 7am when the explosion rocked the ground like an earthquake. Huge flames followed by smoke shot up into the sky. Smoke from the explosion darkened the sky.

Soon after the explosion, men on ATVs roared down the path from the transportation building.

Justin waited as they passed. When they were well past him, Justin lit the fuse to the explosives he had placed on both sides of the path. Then he moved deeper into the woods and closer to the transportation building to watch.

When the explosion around the path occurred, four large trees toppled onto the pathway, completely blocking it. That was exactly what he intended to do.

The ATVs would not be able to use the path to get back to the transportation building. The men would need to go on foot through the woods or take the long way around to campus. Either way, it would buy Justin more time.

He moved to the first set of explosives that he had buried near the front edge of the transportation parking lot. From there, he could see three security guards outside in the parking lot looking at the flames shooting up in the sky for the burned-out meth lab.

Justin lit the fuse for the explosives he had buried near the edge of the parking lot. The wick was long and provided him plenty of time to reach the second set of explosives he had buried near the side of the building. He lit that fuse too. Then, he ran through the woods to an area near the rear of the transportation building and watched.

The explosives near the parking lot went off first. Trees toppled, one falling onto a bus parked near the outer edge of the parking lot. The three security guards scrambled to that area. About a minute later, the second explosion occurred near the side of the building. The impact shattered several windows on one side of the building.

From Justin's viewpoint, he could see one of the security guards talking into a walkie-talkie. The other two were surveying the damage.

Justin didn't know if anyone was inside the building. He didn't see any movement from his view of the windows. He knew that he had very little time to act. People would be coming soon.

He ran to the back of the building, broke out the remaining glass from one of the shattered windows and crawled inside. He didn't see or hear anyone inside the transportation building.

Quickly but quietly, he worked his way inside to the hidden room. He pulled the key from his pocket, put it inside the lock and turned it. The door didn't open. He tried again but failed to open the door. *They must have changed locks*, Justin thought.

Deciding that there was no way he was going to get in that room, he placed the dynamite in several places near the door and outer wall of the hidden room. He lit the fuse and climbed out the window. Then he ran toward the woods. Just as he got to the tree line, the explosion rocked the ground, and he fell hard, hitting his head on a rock laying on the ground.

He was out cold.

CHAPTER 14
THE CAGE

When Justin woke up, he was completely in the dark. The back of his head felt like a knife was piercing it. It hurt like hell. It took him a few seconds to adjust to his surroundings. He wasn't in the woods. Underneath him was concrete. On every side of him and above him were the wires of a cage.

His head was bandaged. He reached into his pocket. The gun he had been carrying was gone. He tried to stand up. But couldn't. The space he was confined to wouldn't allow it. That's when it dawned on him. He was in a cage.

The area he was in was cold and damp. Small drops of water were dripping from above him. His first thoughts were that he was buried somewhere, perhaps in a cave or an abandoned mine. The Ozark hills were full of those. He screamed. But his screams became echoes. He was underground. Justin was certain of that. There was barely enough room for him to turn his body.

He pushed the cage door with all his might. It wouldn't budge. The door was locked. He moved his hands around every part of the cage, searching for any openings or weak spots. There were none. He was trapped like an animal.

The intense darkness was frightening. He took long, slow, deep breaths trying not to panic.

Have I been buried alive? Justin wondered. *Am I deep in the woods, hidden from others, left there to die?* An awful feeling came over him. He had no water, no food and no way out. *This would be a terrible way to die*, he thought.

Justin tried to focus on good thoughts. *Someone bandaged my head. That person must want to keep me alive.*

Then he heard a sound. It sounded like a door being opened. That was when he saw the ray of light that broke through the darkness. At first, the light burned his eyes. He needed time to adjust to it. The light shined directly on him. He squinted his eyes to see where it was coming from. There was a shadowy figure behind the light. He couldn't make out the person, only their silhouette.

"I brought you some food and bottled water," a female voice said.

From behind her, a man's voice said, "Turn over on your back and lift your hands to the top of the cage and leave them there."

"Who are you?" Justin asked.

"It's your buddy, Earl," he said. "Now, shut up and do as you were told."

Justin turned over on his back and lifted his hands.

"Good boy," Earl said. "Now, don't move."

Justin could hear the cage door opening. That's when he saw Risa put a sandwich down inside the cage along with a bottle of water. She backed out of the cage, and Earl shut and locked the cage door.

"Eat up, buddy. You're going to need your strength," Earl said before locking the cage door and backing out of the room.

Risa stayed behind just outside the cage. "I'm so sorry for the loss of your father and everything that has happened to you, Justin. I never wanted you to get hurt. I still love you, Justin. But I'm afraid that I can't help you anymore. By blowing up the meth lab and the transportation building, you've made a lot of powerful and dangerous people angry. They want you to tell them who else knows about the drugs. They want to know if you are working with anyone else. They know that Clay helped you. They want to know where he is. These are extremely bad people, Justin. I'm afraid they are going to make you suffer if you don't tell them what they want to know."

"Where am I, Risa?" Justin asked.

"You're in the basement of the condominium, in the room hidden in the ground. They brought you here after they found you unconscious in the woods. I bandaged your head."

"Are you involved with the drugs, Risa?"

"No, I detest drugs. I hate what they are doing. But I'm afraid there is nothing that I can do about it. I am as much of a prisoner as you are. I lost their trust when I cheated on Richard with you. The only reason they keep me alive is because Richard won't let them harm me. I'm safe as long as Richard is here. He assured them I didn't tell you anything about the drugs. He assured them that I would keep quiet, that he could control me."

"How is Richard involved?" Justin asked.

"I don't know exactly. He's a good man. I've known him since I was in middle school. He would never hurt me or intentionally put me in danger. Maybe that's why he refuses to talk about the drugs or the people he is involved with. I've got to think that he was misled, that he didn't know what he was getting involved with. Richard has never taken drugs. He detests them as much as I do."

"Risa, what about Earl? How is he involved?" Justin asked.

"I don't know. The first time I saw him was a few days ago, at a party in the condo. I thought he was a friend of Karl Gholson, but I really don't know. Like I said, they don't share any information with me."

"Can you help me get out of here, Risa?"

"No. I'm afraid there is no way out of the jam you are in.

They only allowed me to come down here to persuade you to cooperate with them. Tell them everything they want to know. Otherwise, I'm sure they are going to hurt you. I wish there was something I could do for you, Justin, but if I help you, then I will jeopardize my own life. I hope you understand. Please tell them everything you know. They promised me that they wouldn't hurt you if you cooperate."

"Do you really believe that, Risa?"

"I want to. Like I told you, Justin. I still love you." Then Risa left, shutting and locking the door behind her.

Justin was left completely in the dark, cold, afraid and confused. Risa didn't love him. He was certain of that. Maybe she had feelings for him, but it certainly wasn't love. She loved Richard. He was the one she had chosen. Justin was no more than a port in the storm. He was a way of getting back at Richard. Maybe she was mad at him. Maybe she was hurt by him. Whatever it was, she used Justin to get back at him. And now, because of his relationship with Risa, he was in danger. His life was being threatened, and his father had been murdered.

No, that isn't fair to her, Justin told himself. "She isn't responsible for the trouble I'm in. She is in nearly as much danger as I am. She is trapped in an unwinnable situation. She fell in love with the wrong person. Richard had put her life in danger. Now she had no way out. She had to do what she was told.

Still, Justin could never have feelings for her again. Instead of putting her trust in him, she had chosen Richard. She may not have been involved in the drug trade on campus, but her boyfriend was.

Justin laid on the cold concrete floor. He had no blanket to keep him warm. He could barely move. The peanut butter sandwich Risa had left him was soggy from the raindrops coming down from cracks in the ceiling. He ate it anyway. He was starving. He drank some of his water and left the remainder for later. He turned his thoughts from Risa to his mother. She had to be worried sick about him by now. She had lost her husband just a few days earlier, and now she had to be thinking that she might lose her son too. It had to occur to his mother that Justin went back to Branson to seek revenge for the murder of his father. The fact that she hadn't heard back from him since he left had to be weighing heavy on her.

Sometime later, his thoughts turned into dreams, and he fell asleep.

He was awakened abruptly several hours later when his cage door was opened, and he was dragged out by his feet. He was taken to a room on the other side of the basement. The door was opened, and inside stood Sheriff Roscoe Dale.

"Sit him at the table, boys," he said to the two men.

"Should we handcuff him, Sheriff?" one of the men asked.

"Naw, I don't think they'll be a need for that," he said. "I think Mr. Wade wants to cooperate. Isn't that right, Mr. Wade?"

Justin nodded.

"Can the boys get you a cup of coffee, Mr. Wade?

"No thanks," Justin said.

"Suit yourself."

"We'll be right outside if you need us, Sheriff," one of the men said as he exited the room and shut the door.

"Well, Justin, you've caused us quite a bit of trouble, not to mention a lot of money," the Sheriff said. "I got to tell ya, some of my associates didn't want us to bring you back alive from the woods. They aren't very forgiving of people that try to hurt their business. I'm afraid it was some of those people that took care of your daddy last week. I'm sure that you realize that car bomb was meant for you. I had to persuade them that you're more valuable alive right now than you are dead. But I doubt that I will be able to continue to persuade them if you refuse to cooperate. Do you understand, Justin?" Justin nodded his head. "Good. We'll start with a few simple questions. Do you know where your friend Clay is?"

"No. I told him to run after the explosion at the lab," Justin replied.

"Well, come on, Justin. You must have some idea where he went. I'm thinking you two must have talked about what you would do after you blew the hell out of our property."

"We talked about going to the police. I don't know that he would go to the local police, for good reason, so I figure he would have gone to Springfield or someplace like that."

"How did he plan to get out of town?"

"We stole a truck in Branson. The doors were unlocked, and the keys were in it. I assume that's how he got out of town."

"Yeah, that was Lester Calhoun's Ford pickup. He reported it stolen a little after you took it. We found the truck abandoned on the north side of town last night."

"Well, maybe he stole another car."

"Yeah, maybe. But I don't think so. Branson's a small town. If he stole a local's car, they would have surely reported it to me by now. Do you have someone else working with you boys?"

"No, we were by ourselves."

"Where'd you get the explosives?"

"There's a construction area north of town where the State stores dynamite to blow up mountain boulders to clear the way for the new highway."

"Yeah, that's what I figured. Tell me who you told about the drug operation."

"I didn't tell anyone. Karl Gholson told me not to. So did Richard."

"Come on, son. You don't really expect me to buy that, do you? Who did you talk to?"

"I talked to three of my teammates, the three that were with me the night we broke into the transportation building."

"Yes, we know about them. As I'm sure you know by now, Earl is one of us. He shared everything you talked about. Your other two friends have been dealt with. It's safe to say they won't be talking to anyone."

"Who else have you talked to, Justin?"

"I talked to Risa. But you know that."

"Yes, we know that. Son, you're not very good at picking girlfriends, are you?"

"Speaking of that, what did you tell your girlfriend in Kansas City? I believe her name is Elise, isn't it? Did you tell her about Risa? I bet you didn't share with her that you slept with Risa, did you? I don't think she'd be very understanding, do you? Did you happen to tell her about what you saw in the woods or what you found in the transportation building? Did you tell her about the money you made from the drug run to St. Louis?"

"No, she doesn't know anything. We broke up before I started at S of O. She's dating someone else now."

"Oh, Justin, I was hoping you wouldn't lie to me." Then Sheriff McClain raised his fist and hit Justin with all his force in the right jaw. Justin went tumbling off the chair, landing on the concrete floor. "Don't lie to me again, boy. I won't be so gentle to you next time," he said, lifting Justin up and sitting him back in the chair.

"I know you two were together the night your dad was killed. Did you tell her anything about us or the drugs?"

"No, I swear. I didn't want to get her involved."

"How about her daddy? He's a captain on the Kansas City police force. Did you tell her daddy, son?"

"No, I didn't tell him anything."

"I hope you're right, son. I'd hate to mess up her pretty face. You should know that we have eyes watching her and your mother and brother too."

Justin looked shocked that he mentioned his mother and

Brian. "Don't look so surprised, son. We know Elise's daddy moved your family to a safe house, and we know exactly where it is."

That statement struck a nerve with Justin. His only hope of surviving was that Clay was able to escape to Kansas City and tell Elise's dad what was going on. But, if the Sheriff was right and someone was watching Elise's house and the safe house, then Clay, Elise and his family were all in danger.

"What did you take from the transportation building the night you broke into it?" Sheriff McClain asked.

"Just the key to the hidden room. That's the only thing I took, and you got that back from my dormitory room."

"That is consistent with what Earl told me. Son, I believe you are telling me the truth. I want you to know that if it was up to me, I would make your death quick. You wouldn't suffer. But unfortunately, you upset some very powerful people. They aren't as understanding as me. They want you to suffer. The end result will be the same, but they insist that your death be slow and painful."

"Can you answer one question for me, Sheriff?"

"Depends on what that question is."

"How is Earl Myers involved?"

"Yeah, he really fooled you, didn't he?" Roscoe said with a smile. "It's his property that the meth lab is built on. He's the nephew of Karl Gholson. His older brother, Jason, is the head of campus security. Hell, son, they run the whole operation."

That's when the sheriff yelled for the two men that had been waiting outside the door to come back in.

"Son, these boys are going to take you back to the cage. But, first, the people you hurt by destroying the lab and the transportation building insist that I give you a message of their displeasure with you."

Roscoe signaled to the two men entering the room. They

grabbed Justin's arms and lifted him out of his chair. Roscoe moved a wicker chair to the corner of the room. Then he cut the wicker out of the seat portion of the chair with a sharp knife. The two men put handcuffs on Justin's hands and moved him to the wicker chair. They placed a large block of wood between Justin's feet and ankles so he could not close his legs.

Roscoe opened the desk drawer and pulled out a rope approximately three feet long. Attached to the end of the rope was a baseball.

"This will be very painful, son. But only for a few seconds. Then you'll pass out. But I'm afraid that pain is going to stay with you for a long time," Roscoe said with a smile as he moved directly in front of Justin. "Hope you're not planning on using your Johnson for a while, son," he said with a chuckle.

Roscoe swung the rope several times, gaining momentum with each swing. Then he swung the ball between Justin's legs and directly into his ball sack with such force he could hear a crack. Justin's screams shook the walls. A few seconds later, he passed out.

When he awoke hours later, the pain was intense, so intense that his legs had gone numb from the pain. Through his tears, he could tell that he was back in the cage. The area was completely dark. He had no idea how long he was unconscious nor whether it was daytime or nighttime. He laid in agony for several hours when he heard the door open and saw the light from the basement. Standing in front of the cage, carrying a paper plate of scrambled eggs and a plastic bottle of water, was Risa.

She opened the cage door and put the food and water down in front of Justin. Then she shut and locked the cage door. "Eat the eggs. You'll feel better," she said. "I put some pain pills inside them," she whispered. "I'm so sorry, Justin. I wish there was something I could do. Eat the eggs. Then, try to sleep," she said as she walked out of the room, locking the door behind her.

After eating the eggs, the pain softened. He got tired and fell asleep. He dreamed of his high school days, his running, his friends, his family and Elise. He thought about his dad and the good times they had. He thought about what his life would have been like had he never decided to come to S of O, had he never met Risa. He thought about the wonderful life he had just a few months earlier. He dreamed of escaping and going back home. He dreamed of being able to start his life over, of being able to make different decisions, of being able to take a different fork in the road. He wished that everything he had gone through was no more than a nightmare he would soon awaken from.

His sleep was interrupted abruptly when a bucket of ice water was thrown on his head.

"Get up, son. It's playtime again," Roscoe said, laughing.

Two men dragged him out of the cage, into the basement and back to the secret room. They sat him in a chair next to a table and handcuffed his right hand to the leg of the table. Then, they tied his legs to the chair so he couldn't move. For a few seconds, the intense pain he had was interrupted by the fear he had for what was coming next.

Roscoe sat down at the desk opposite Justin and smiled. Then he pulled out a metal instrument that looked like thin metal pliers on one side and a flat-head screwdriver with a sharp blade on the other. "Bet you've never seen one of these before, have you, son?" he said with a smile. "It's a very effective tool for peeling back fingernails and removing the nail right down to the skin. Did you know that there are more sensitive nerves located in the raw skin underneath a fingernail than in almost any other part of the body? I understand that peeling back a fingernail is one of the most painful things a person can experience. Now, I don't know that personally, but I'm hoping you can confirm it for me."

Roscoe used the sharp side of the instrument to dig underneath the fingernail. As soon as he began, Justin began to scream in pain. "You know, son, that the most agonizing part of this procedure is that you won't pass out. You'll be awake the entire time to realize the full extent of the pain," Roscoe said.

Once he had dug underneath the nail and just beneath the surface of the skin, he pulled the blade out and turned the instrument around. With the thin, metal pliers, side open, he latched onto the nail, tightened the grasp and twisted the instrument to pull the nail backward.

Justin begged him to stop. He screamed at the top of his lungs. The pain was incredible. Blood flowed from the raw, exposed skin underneath his fingernail.

With one final twist and pull, Roscoe completely removed the fingernail. He duplicated the same procedure for each of the five fingers on Justin's left hand. Once all the nails were removed, exposing the raw, blood-soaked skin underneath, he pulled out a container of salt from his desk drawer.

"I have been told that pouring salt into an open wound causes intense pain that is similar to having a major limb cut off without the benefit of any pain medication. The good thing is that you won't suffer more than a few minutes before you pass out," Roscoe said with a sick smile.

Various types of torture continued every few hours for the next two days. He endured two wisdom teeth pulled out with pliers, sleep deprivation by using intense lights and loud noises, waterboarding and strangulation until he passed out.

Twice every day, Risa appeared at his cage. She brought him food and water. She cried. She prayed with him. She told him how sorry she was that he was suffering the way he was. But she always left, locking the cage and door behind her and giving him no hope of escape.

Sometime on the third day of his captivity, the door was opened, the light shined in from the basement, and he saw Richard and Roscoe standing over him. "Pack your bags, son.

You're going for a trip," Roscoe said.

Ten men coming into the room behind them pulled Justin out of the cage and into the basement. They tried to walk him up the basement stairs, but his legs gave out on him. So, they carried him up the stairs and out the door to a plain, white cargo van inside the garage. They opened up the back of the van and put him in. Inside the cargo area of the van was a small rowboat. Richard climbed in the back with Justin.

"Just relax," Richard said, pulling out a needle from a small box he was carrying. "This will help you," he said, injecting the needle into Justin's arm.

Roscoe climbed in the front seat of the van along with Karl Gholson. "I thought I'd take this trip with you, Justin," Karl said, looking back at him from the passenger seat. "I warned you a while back that you should play ball, that you shouldn't cause any waves. You have no one to blame but yourself for the situation you're in."

Roscoe started the engine, and the van rolled out of the garage. It was dark outside. It was the first time in three days that Justin had any idea what time of day it was.

The moon was behind the clouds that night. A soft, gentle rain came down. A low-hanging fog came off the lake's surface and made visibility difficult.

That night reminded Justin of the evening he saw the boys being pulled from the campus pond, the night he saw the blood in the fountain.

As the van drove the side roads toward campus, the rain intensified. Thunder, followed by lightning, came over the mountains to the north of the campus. The squeaking sound of worn windshield wipers on high speed echoed over the sound of heavy rain slamming with the roof and sides of the van.

"It's a good night for a swim, don't you think, Mr. Wade?" Roscoe said from the driver's seat.

The van stopped briefly as it entered the gates at the top of the hill at the entrance to campus.

"Go on in," he heard a security guard say as the van began to move through the gates and onto campus.

The lights on the lamp posts throughout the campus were on, although their glow was blurred through the dense fog.

The students must be back from Christmas break, Justin thought. *But it must be the middle of the night. The dorms are probably locked, and most of the students are sound asleep.*

Justin could see the glow of the fountain lights off to the left side as the van came to a stop. He felt funny. Whatever Richard shot into his veins was beginning to take hold. His entire body was warm. He could barely move his legs and his arms. They felt so heavy. He tried with all his strength to move them. He couldn't. It was as if his entire body was paralyzed. He tried to close his eyes, but his eyelids wouldn't move. It was impossible for him to control any part of his body.

The van stopped. The engine was turned off, and the headlights went dark. A few seconds later, the back door to the van opened up. The rain was coming down in sheets now, pouring into the van and onto Justin. But he couldn't feel a thing.

Richard grabbed Justin underneath his armpits. Roscoe grabbed his legs. They lifted him up and out of the van onto the muddy ground.

"Damn, it's cold out here," Karl complained.

Justin didn't feel the cold. His body was completely numb. He didn't even feel the rain pounding down on him. His hearing was fine, though. He heard everything that was said. He heard the rain pounding down around him. He heard the clamor of thunder from the skies around him.

His eyesight was fine too. He saw the rain, the bolts of lightning, the lights from the fountain and his killers.

Richard pulled the boat out of the van, and with Roscoe's

help, he carried it to the edge of the pond. Karl Gholson stayed behind with Justin.

"You know, I really liked you, Justin. In a way, you reminded me of myself, strong-willed, determined and smart. The problem is you never learned what side of the bread to put the butter. If you'd only played ball with us, you might have gone a long way," he said.

A few minutes later, Richard and Roscoe came back. They lifted Justin off the ground and began to carry him to the pond.

"Aren't you coming, Karl?" Roscoe asked.

"Yeah, just give me a minute. I've got to put another coat on. It's too freaking cold out here." Karl got in the van, grabbed a heavier coat that he had brought with him from the condo and hurried to the pond just as Justin was placed in the rowboat.

The three men lifted the boat and placed it in the water. Then, Roscoe climbed in the front of the boat.

"Come on, Karl. You wanted to be a part of this. Get in the boat," Roscoe yelled.

Karl climbed in the back, and Richard pushed the boat from the shore just enough to get it moving toward the fountain.

Roscoe rowed the boat to an area just in front of the fountain. He stopped there.

"Do you have any last words to say, son?"

"Justin looked up at Roscoe and defiantly said, "Fuck you."

"Help me lift him up, Karl," Roscoe said.

They lifted Justin up, causing the boat to rock back and forth. Karl lost his balance and fell into the water.

"Damn, I guess I've got to do it by myself," Roscoe said. Then he lifted Justin to the edge of the boat and pushed him. As he fell into the water, Justin managed to curl his left leg slightly around Roscoe's right ankle. The sheriff staggered slightly and lost his balance falling over the edge of the boat and hitting his head on a sharp corner of the boat as he fell into the water.

The shot that Richard had given him had mostly paralyzed Justin's body. He could barely move. He couldn't swim. His body slowly went down to the bottom of the pound. He held his breath as long as he possibly could.

A bolt of lightning struck a tree just after Justin entered the water. The tree fell on a power line, the power line fell to the ground, and the entire campus went dark. The fountain lights went off, and the sprays of water stopped.

From the shore, Richard heard the sirens coming closer. He took off his shoes and jumped into the water, swimming to the area in front of the fountain where Roscoe and Justin fell in. When he reached the area where they went under, he dove toward the bottom of the pond.

There were over two dozen police cars and unmarked cars that raced onto campus that night. Karl was captured swimming back to shore.

The sirens, flashing lights and commotion around the pond woke most of the students. They exited their dorms and headed to the pond area. Yellow police tape stopped them from getting very close. Rescue boats and divers entered the water to search for survivors. But it was just too dark, and the fog was too dense to see anything.

The electric company worked frantically to get the line fixed and the lights back on. When they did, the fountain began to spray again. Just as it started, a loud grinding noise began, and within seconds the fountain water turned from white to red.

CHAPTER 15
A FINAL FAREWELL

Clay returned to S of O on the day of the funeral. He returned with no fanfare. The students at S of O blamed him for the bad publicity the school was receiving. The school administration had no use for him. They wished he'd never come back.

In reality, Clay didn't expose the drugs and corruption on campus. The FBI was already aware of what was going on. They had someone on the inside, someone that knew every detail of the drug operation, someone that knew everyone that was involved.

But the identity of that person was not revealed, nor would it ever be revealed.

Clay was the one that got the credit and the blame for bringing the FBI to the campus for exposing the drug trade. After blowing up the meth lab, Clay drove back to Kansas City. He made it to Elise's house. He alerted her father to what had happened on campus. Elise's father contacted his friend with the FBI. It just so happened that the FBI was only days away from breaking the case anyway. Clay only expedited that process.

Associates with the Kansas City mob were arrested the next day. One, a hitman, was arrested outside Elise's home. Another was arrested outside the safe house where Justin's mother and brother were staying.

The FBI and State police raced to the S of O campus when the person on the inside alerted them that Justin was about to be murdered. Drugs were found in a safe hidden in the athletic building on campus. Karl Gholson had the safe moved to a hidden room next to his office after the transportation building was blown up. Also, in the safe was a ledger exposing their sales network.

The drugs were scheduled to be loaded on a bus taking the basketball team to a tournament in Chicago on January 2. But after the explosion, the trip was cancelled, forcing the group to hide the drugs in a safe place.

Local and national news networks blanketed the campus. The drug operation was the leading story on most networks for several days. This became an embarrassment of epic proportions to a school that prided itself on its conservative, Christian values.

Clay came back to S of O that day, knowing that he was hated by most of the people on the campus. He came back as a sign of defiance. He didn't give a rat's ass for that school anymore. But he did care deeply for his freedom to do what he wanted to do. He was committed to graduating from college, to make something of himself. For all its faults, despite all the bad memories S of O gave him, they provided a free education. He couldn't afford to go to any other school. Besides, he needed to make a statement to others that they couldn't force him out, that they couldn't intimidate him, and that he wasn't afraid of them.

Visitors flocked to the campus on the day of the funeral. Television crews were everywhere. Flags flew at half-mast that day. The funeral was held in the campus church. It was, by far, the largest church in the area. Still, three hours before the funeral service, every seat had been taken. Overflow crowds were seated in the vestibule, and after that area was full, seats were set up outside of the church and in the gymnasium, where television monitors provided the service.

Clay wouldn't go to the funeral that day. He couldn't. The wounds of what had happened ran too deep. He couldn't understand why people treated the man like a hero and why so many people were sad about his death. They didn't know the dark side of him. Or, if they did, they chose to ignore it.

Sheriff Roscoe Dale may have died a hero in the minds of the hill people of the Branson area. But Clay knew him for what he really was, a sadistic murderer.

The local news media had spun the story that the local sheriff had been the hero, that he died trying to stop the drug operation. The national news media told a completely different story about the sheriff. They exposed him as corrupt and a sadistic murderer.

But the hill people had never trusted outsiders. They chose not to believe the national media. They chose to believe that Sherriff Roscoe McClain died a hero. The funeral lasted for nearly two hours. Dozens of people spoke. The entire S of O choir was present to sing nearly a dozen gospel hymns. Near the end of the service, thick, dark clouds descended on the area. The wind picked up, and the rain began, slowly at first and then turning into a downpour.

After the funeral service, the casket was carried to a hearse, and a long funeral procession began snaking its way through the back roads leading to the Branson Cemetery. Hundreds of people stood in the pouring rain on the sides of the road to pay their respect.

The funeral and procession to the cemetery after were fitting of a hero.

Clay spent his first day back on campus in his room, the same room he used to share with Justin. He was alone now. He was lonely, but he would never let anyone see that side of him. He had decided the night of the drowning in the pond that he would not let S of O ever get the best of him. He had decided that night that he would return to the campus, that he would graduate and that he would make something out of himself.

It wasn't going to be easy. He would not have his best friend with him. Everyone on campus seemed to hate him right now.

Maybe, with time, he thought, *people will understand what I did. Or, maybe with time, they will forget.*

S of O would be better off for what Justin and Clay had done, but no one could see that right now. The school would not only survive, but it would thrive in the years to come. The memories of the bodies in the pond and the blood in the fountain would fade and eventually disappear.

The pond and its fountain would remain the centerpiece of the campus. It would continue to be a gathering place for students and faculty on warm summer nights and cool fall evenings.

Clay graduated from S of O three years later with a degree in criminal justice. His mother passed away during his senior year, and his brother was sent to prison for trafficking drugs. He had only one person show up for his graduation, a friend from the past.

His hopes of people forgetting and forgiving him never came to fruition while he remained on the campus. He was a loner those three years. He never had another roommate. But, for the most part, people left him alone. He learned to enjoy the solitude, or maybe he just learned to accept it.

There was no way in hell that he was going to quit, that he was going to leave school. After graduation, Clay went to work for the FBI. He would have a great deal of success over the coming years. He would find love and marry. He would have three children, a boy and two girls. Clay left the campus of S of O the day he graduated, and he never returned.

***

The wedding in Sikeston, MO, was huge. It was a wonderful May day, with not a cloud in the sky and perfect late spring temperatures.

Risa was a beautiful bride. She had been dreaming of this day since she was in middle school. She had been planning it for over a year. She was completely and absolutely in love. She knew soon after her first date with him that he was the man she would marry someday. He felt the same way about her.

She never went back to S of O. Instead, she went to Southeast Missouri State and graduated three years later with a teaching degree. Soon after graduation, she landed a teaching job in Sikeston. That was a good thing. Risa had no interest in living anywhere else. She was born and raised in Sikeston, and her family and friends were there.

The groom had graduated a year early and had taken a position with the Sikeston Daily News. He proposed to Risa two days later.

Richard had never loved anyone else. He had never even dated anyone else. The two of them were meant to be together. They had always been meant to be together.

But there was a time that she nearly left him. That was during her freshman year at S of O when she met a handsome boy named Justin. She fell in love with him for a brief time.

Richard had become withdrawn. She noticed that shortly after starting school at S of O. He was more secretive then and more distant. He worried about her more than before, and he had become controlling. It was that behavior that caused her to run into the arms of Justin.

He fell in love with her. Her love for him was real, but it wasn't as strong as the love she had for Richard.

She never realized that Richard was involved in drugs. She only knew that he was in trouble and that he needed her. He kept her at the condominium for her protection. She had lost the trust of some of his associates because of her relationship with Justin.

She could have escaped the condo on numerous occasions.

She stayed there for Richard's sake because he wanted her to.

When the FBI raided the condo, they took Risa into custody. But she didn't go to jail. Instead, she was taken into witness protection. Richard joined her a few days later.

That was when she found out that Richard had been working with the FBI. He was responsible for bringing down the drug operation in Branson. He was the informer. He was the hero. But no one other than Risa would ever know it.

***

Winters on the campus of Missouri Western in St. Joseph, MO, were brutal. The campus was located on top of a large hill on the east side of town. It was a relatively new school with few trees to block the strong winds that were prevalent in that area during the late fall and winter months.

Snow drifted with the winds, and temperatures fell below zero on many days. It was not a very forgiving place during those winter months. But winter gave way to spring and spring to summer, and when classes began again in late August, the campus took on new life.

Two lovers were joined together again. He had been alone during those cold, lonely nights of winter. Now he was with the one he loved. He had waited a long time for this moment, for the time they could walk hand and hand through campus, free and together, at last.

He had nearly drowned that cold November night in the pond. His lungs had taken in water. He had stopped breathing. But Richard jumped into the water. He dove down and pulled Justin's lifeless body to the shore. Paramedics worked on him for several minutes. They transported him to the Branson hospital. He was in intensive care for nearly a week. When he awoke, Elise was sitting next to him, holding his hand tightly.

When she graduated from high school, there was only one college she applied to. It was the one where her boyfriend went.

They were both happy now, content with their lives and looking forward to their future together.

Justin went back to S of O one more time. It was to attend his best friend's graduation. It was the first time the two of them had seen each other since the night the meth lab was blown up. After the graduation, they walked the paths through campus one last time, ending at the edge of the pond, near the fountain. They sat on the bench where Justin had met Risa long ago. They sat silently and drank a beer together, looking out at the fountain, shooting streams of water high into the air and arching them back down to the surface of the pond, where they created ripples that flowed to the shore. The pond was once Justin's favorite spot to go. It was peaceful, tranquil, and a place of beauty. But that's not what Justin saw that day. He only saw a symbol of an outward beauty that, inside, resided so many secrets and so much pain.

Both boys needed that quiet time at the pond together to remind them of what was most important in life, to remind them of why they could never let the past control their future.

They were the best man at each other's weddings. Justin and Elise married two years after graduating from Missouri Western. They had four children, one boy and three girls. Justin never told his children about S of O and the fountain. He never told them about the murders, about the blood in the fountain, and he never went back to S of O again.

The fog still comes over the lake and swallows the surrounding valley, including the campus of S of O. But it's a gentle fog. It comes in slowly, and when it leaves, the sun always seems to shine. The hills that surround the school hide many secrets. The hill people that live there guard those secrets. For a brief period of time, S of O played a prominent role in guarding those secrets. When they were exposed, it damaged their reputation, but only for a short period of time.

The school has prospered over the years. The students that

go there receive a free education, a quality education. Everyone that goes to school there still works on campus. Their work is exchanged for a free education. It's a unique place, nestled in the hills of the Ozarks, a beautiful, tranquil area where people work hard and are God-fearing. The pace of the Ozarks is slow. Warm, green summers give way to the cool, crisp days of Fall. The leaves on the trees change to the bright amber and orange colors of autumn. The three lakes surrounding the area turn majestic and quiet in the fall. Tourists have gone. Traffic is over. The lakes begin their slumber.

As the sun sets behind the mountains, a warm glow of colors shines down on the valley below, bouncing off the surface of the water and resulting in a rainbow of colors. This is a slice of heaven that few people ever see. It is what makes the Ozarks one of the most majestic places.

But long after the sun has set, after the dorms have been locked and the students are asleep, the cool temperatures of fall collide with the warm waters of the lakes and the fog creeps in, the winds pick up, and the echoes of the past can be heard between the ripples on the surface of the pond.

And, if you look long enough, you can almost see the white sprays of water jetting up from the fountain turn to red.

-THE END-

Alan Brown grew up in the suburbs of Kansas City and graduated from Shawnee Mission East High School in 1973 and Avila University in 1979. Now He lives in a suburb of St. Louis, MO, with my wife and three daughters. He also has four sons that are grown and living outside the home. He enjoys writing about his experiences growing up, examining the fantastical side, the dark side of a person's natural fears. All of his books are based on a reality in his life. He is a fan of Alfred Hitchcock. Like his stories, Alan Brown's will conclude with a twist, something he hopes will take the reader by surprise.

www.ingramcontent.com/pod-product-compliance
Lightning Source LLC
Chambersburg PA
CBHW030332180626
46810CB00003B/1324